Bitter RIVALS

by

J. Sterling

BITTER RIVALS

Edited by:

Jovana Shirley, Unforeseen Editing

Cover Design by:

Michelle Preast at Indie Book Covers

ISBN-13: 978-1-945042-20-1 (Inspire Magic)

Thank you for purchasing this book.

Sign up for my personal newsletter to get e-mails about new releases and sales right to your inbox:

http://tinyurl.com/SterlingNewsletter

Never miss a new release again! Sign up for text messages:

Text: Jack

To: 77948

Please visit the author's website

www.j-sterling.com

to find out where additional versions may be purchased.

Dedication

For my Mom- who never hesitates to tell me how proud she is of me, understands how hard I work, and claims to love everything I write. Your support and belief in me is invaluable. Thank you.

MY NEMESIS

Julia

"LOOK AT THE number of women standing there fawning all over him," my assistant and best friend since grade school said, her head shaking, as she pointed a finger at my archnemesis across the room. "I'm actually embarrassed to be female right now."

I pushed her arm down before he noticed and did something mortifying in response, like inform the entire room that I was in love with him or something. I wouldn't put it past him. James Russo loved to embarrass and humiliate me. He'd been doing it since high school.

"Jeanine! Don't draw his attention toward us. And I don't want to look at him, or his fan club." I groaned even though it was a lie, and she damn well knew it.

James Russo had grown up to be one hell of a gorgeous man. And I absolutely wanted to check him out, maybe even lose myself in a dirty fantasy or two, but I couldn't admit that part. At least, not out loud. I was supposed to loathe his very existence. Despising James was as much a part of my DNA as my dark hair and Italian heritage.

"You totally want to look at him," she teased. "Maybe then you'll see how often he looks at you."

Pivoting on my brand-new high heel, I turned to face my soon-to-be-former best friend if she didn't pull it together, "James Russo does not look at me any more than I look at him. We hate each other, and you know this. You've always known this. He is the world's worst human. If there were an award for it, he'd win. Why are you being so weird? Are you drunk?" I glanced around her at our stash of wine bottles still firmly in place on the ground, checking to make sure none were empty.

If anyone knew how much James and I couldn't stand one another, it was Jeanine. She had grown up with the two of us, had been fully aware of our families' mutual war, and had been caught in the middle of it on more than one occasion. While she sometimes placated me with subtle jabs and insults in James's honor, she usually played the role of peacekeeper—or at least, she tried.

"I just wonder when you two will bury the hatchet, is all," she said for, like, the fourteen thousandth time since we'd been born.

"Never," I said, giving her the exact same response that I always had.

Burying the hatchet wasn't an option in my family. Even if I wanted to, which I didn't, it wasn't allowed. My dad would disown me completely and make me change my last name before he ever forgave a Russo.

Glancing across the competition space, I spotted James, his dark hair framing his two-week-old stubble as he smiled at a group of women, who, instead of working their own wine booths, looked all too willing to leave and take him to bed if he asked. Not that I cared what James did in his bed or with whom, but damn that facial hair. It would be the death of me. I'd spent one too many nights dreaming of the way it would feel as he dived between my thighs or as he kissed me, brushing across my cheek. That man sure knew how to keep his beard in check—always perfectly trimmed, fading just right toward the top where it met his hairline. It annoyed me as much as it turned me on, which was saying a lot since he was the most annoying human in existence.

"You've got a little drool right there." Jeanine nudged me with her arm, pointing at the corner of her mouth, and I snarled.

"I'm just wondering why he keeps coming to these things when he knows he's going to lose. Do you think he comes to meet women?" I reached for a case of our wine and started pulling out the bottles one at a time, so Jeanine could uncork them and fill the waiting glasses.

She laughed so hard at my question that she choked. "Like he needs to come here to meet women. Besides, the only woman he wants is you. Why do you think he's never stayed in a long-term relationship before? Probably for the same reason all yours have failed."

My eyes felt like they bugged straight out of my head and rolled onto the floor under the table. "What are you even talking about right now?" I looked at my best friend like she had grown two heads. "My relationships don't fail,"

I said a little too defensively. "I mean, it's not my fault that every guy I've dated seems to be more interested in my winery than they are in me."

"You don't even give them a chance. They're out of the running before they even start the race. One wrong word, and you cut them off. Deem them unworthy. And we both know it's because you want the one guy you can't have. You're just too stubborn or scared to admit it."

My mouth snapped shut in response, wanting to argue, to fight back, but unsure of what the hell to say in response to that. So, I maneuvered the subject away from me and back to *him*. "James has never had a serious relationship? What do you call Maria? And when he dated that one girl from Seattle last year?"

I remembered when I'd learned about his long-distance girlfriend and how jealous I'd become, my stomach churning at the assumption that if James were dating someone out of state, it meant he was super serious about her. My imagination had soared as I braced myself for the news that they were engaged. I had been so relieved when I heard they'd broken up.

"Maria lasted a whopping six months. That's not long-term, sorry. Plus, I heard, the second she wanted more, started pressing him for a commitment and a future, he broke up with her and never looked back. And the girl from Seattle was just that—a girl so far away that he never had to fully commit to her. The man is waiting for you, the same way he's always been."

It was my turn to choke on laughter. "The man probably just wants to steal my recipes and get into my head to see how I come up with ideas and to see which wine I'm entering this year so that he can copy it for next month's competition." *It is a 2012 Chianti with hints of cinnamon, by the way. It has never been done before in our region, and I perfected the hell out of it. James Russo couldn't copy my wine if he tried.*

"You're insane," Jeanine said. "But, back to the original question, we both know that James comes here because it's his job and he has to. The same way you do," she said a little too snarkily for my liking.

I was the face of La Bella Wines. Not literally. I mean, my face wasn't plastered on the company logo or the wine labels, thank God, but when it came to marketing, events, fundraisers and competitions, I was the person who came to mind when you thought of my family's award-winning winery. The same way that James Russo was the face of his less-award-winning one.

While I focused on bringing something different to La Bella Wines with each season, James seemed content to focus on coming in second place year after year. He should be used to it by now, but that man never quit or gave up. Whenever competition season rolled around, he assaulted me with verbal jabs, testing my patience and swearing that this would be the year his wine would outperform mine. It never was. And it never would be. Not as long as I was still breathing.

"I don't have to do this. I choose to," I reminded Jeanine as I uncorked the various bottles since she hadn't even started doing it yet.

"Well, so does James. He doesn't have to either. He wants to."

Was she actually defending him to me right now?

"Since when do you know so much about James's personal life, thoughts, and opinions?"

Nerves shot through my body, and my core tensed up at the sudden thought that my best friend and my archnemesis might be hooking up behind my back. Why else would she argue with me about him of all people?

"Are you two …" I couldn't even finish the question without wanting to throw up at the betrayal.

"What? No! Like I would ever do that to you!" she exclaimed.

I felt my entire body relax. "Right. You wouldn't date my enemy because you know I'd have to fire you and never speak to you again."

She finally started doing her job, filling up the empty glasses with our latest wine before placing them in perfect display alignment on the table. "No, Julia. I'd never go after James because, no matter what you try to tell yourself—or me—I know that you have feelings for him. I'd never do that to *you*."

My face flamed, my cheeks heating with either righteous anger or embarrassment on being so blatantly called out—I wasn't sure which. Jeanine knew that despite my family's disapproval, I was attracted to James and had been since he hit puberty sometime during junior high school. I'd only allowed myself to admit it out loud to her one time, but that one time had apparently been all she needed since she liked to throw it in my face every now and then.

"I don't," I stuttered, "have feelings for that jerk."

"Uh-huh." She rolled her eyes at me, a glass of wine in one hand as she handed me a half-filled glass with the other.

We each swirled the liquid twice before raising it to our noses and sipping slowly. The moan that escaped my lips was uncontrollable. It was good, really good, like *going to win first place again* good. At least, I hoped it would. Nothing was guaranteed in this business.

"This is amazing. How do you do it?"

I shrugged my shoulders. "Science," I said with a smile because it was half-true.

Making wine *was* a delicate science, but it was also instinct and the willingness to think outside the box and try new things. The majority of local wineries stuck to the old-fashioned, tried-and-true wine blends that practically guaranteed success. Very few had the capacity to risk attempting new flavor combinations without the fear of losing it all or at least taking a huge hit to their profit margin. I understood their concerns, especially when their entire livelihood depended on their wines not only being drinkable, but also profitable.

A handful of years back, I'd convinced my parents to set aside a small portion of our fermenting wine barrels to me, strictly for my experiments. They only agreed because I told them that if I could create a new flavor blend, we could produce and market it as a limited edition, never to be re-created again in the same way. I informed them that it would make the wine fly off the shelves, that customers would flock to our tasting room to try it before it sold out, and that making anything a *limited edition* instantly added value. My only formal request had been that they *had* to let me use the grapes from our south side vines.

The south side was the one part of our winery that frankly didn't make any sense, and we never understood how the vines had even gotten planted in the first place. My great-grandfather must have been insane when he came up with the idea. La Bella land was made up of gentle, rolling hills, but there was one small section that had a steep drop-off, making it extremely hard to harvest. It was basically a cliff—minus the *falling to your death* part, but still a cliff nonetheless.

That section of land produced our best grapes. For whatever reason, that steep hill got exposed to a different sort of weather climate than the rest. The sun seemed to shine a little longer there, and the rain tended to fall a little harder. In return, resulting in a slightly different soil content, and the grapes were unlike any of the other grapes on our land. As a matter of fact, the grapes there were unlike any other grapes in the entire valley. No one was able to replicate what we had created with the south side vines, and trust me, they tried. I always assumed that you couldn't replicate what Mother Nature gave you, but I never blamed them for trying. Those vines were the ones that kept winning all the awards, long before I'd ever started experimenting with them. The south side vines had put La Bella winery on the map, but we'd still be a success without them.

"I really like how you can smell the cinnamon before you can taste it. It's like your nose knows it's there way before your taste buds ever do."

I grinned because that was exactly my plan—making the scent known, but only recognized long after you swallowed. Food pairing was an integral part of running a winery, and it was something I respected and spent a lot of time researching for our customers and business. We had a menu in our tasting room, specifically designed for wine and food pairing—the most popular being what to drink with different types of chocolates and cheeses.

During my research, I had come across an article about a winery in another country putting flavors inside of their wines, and I wondered why we weren't doing that. That was when my desire to experiment had been born. But, instead of inserting multiple flavors into the wine like they were, I only wanted one—one perfectly infused flavor with a singular wine type. I believed that less was more, that we had enough in life to overwhelm our senses. Last year's winner was a limited-edition rich dark chocolate port.

"I'm glad you like it," I said as Jeanine poured herself another glass.

"I don't like it. I love it," she said, finishing it off. "Do you have any new war information?"

"Okay, that's enough for you." I took the bottle from her greedy little hands, and she pouted. "You literally ask me this every single time we see James—which is a lot, you know," I complained, annoyed that she insisted on questioning the decades-old feud instead of accepting it the way I had.

Jeanine knew that if I had learned any new information about our rivalry, I would have told her by now.

"I just think that if you're supposed to hate someone based on their last name alone, you should at least know every single reason. You do realize that this all borders eerily close to *Romeo and Juliet*, right? I mean, you're both even Italian."

"So, I'm what, Juliet in this scenario? And James is Romeo?" I spat out a sick laugh. "I suppose you're my chambermaid? Thanks for letting me die, by the way," I continued to tease.

My parents refused to talk about whatever had happened between our two families in detail. And my dad practically exploded each time I even hinted about wanting to know more than what I'd been told.

"Isn't it enough that I tell you his family almost ruined ours? Why can't you accept that they're evil and if they could, they would take over our vines the second we turned our back to them? Stay away from that Russo boy!"

He always ended his tirade with a warning for me to stay away from James and made me promise that I would. He'd told me on more than one occasion that nothing in this world could disappoint him more than me befriending James Russo and that if it ever happened, he would disown me completely and I'd lose the winery.

That was a pretty damn heavy cross to bear. One I'd never even confessed to my best friend. I kept that tidbit of information inside, too embarrassed to admit it to anyone, not even my mother. It felt like some sort of betrayal to my father to repeat it out loud, especially when he felt so strongly about the subject. Instead, I'd allowed his words to become a part of me, a weight so unbearably heavy at first but, with time, had become manageable. James was the devil who could make me lose the winery and everything I'd worked for my whole life. No one was worth that. End of story.

"Now that we're older, you've never wondered why you're supposed to hate him? I mean, wondered enough to push it and get real answers? At what point do you both deserve the truth?" Jeanine pushed. She was always pushing.

It wasn't that I didn't want to know; it was more that I'd simply accepted the fact that I might never know, and I'd convinced myself that I was okay with that. Even though our entire small town knew about the rivalry, no one ever dared to elaborate on it. I wasn't sure who they were scared of more—my father or James's father. Whenever I'd made the mistake of asking someone who I thought would know details, they always said they couldn't remember or that I should ask my parents. Even old man Johnson at the liquor store had said our families' story was like folklore now, passed down from generation to generation, but all screwed up the way the game of telephone got and that I couldn't trust what anyone around here said about it. I couldn't argue with that logic, so I'd eventually stopped trying.

I groaned before directing my attention once again toward James. "He's a stubborn ass. He's cocky and egotistical, and he thinks the world revolves around him. That's reason enough for me. What about that rumor he started about me in high school? I can't even look at him without wanting to gouge his eyeballs out for that."

"That was a hundred years ago. And I still think he did it on purpose," she countered softly as if scared of my reaction.

"Of course he did it on purpose! He wanted to ruin my life," I practically shouted as my mind took an instant trip down memory lane.

It had been in high school, junior year, and James had told everyone that I had sex with him. Not just sex, but that I had also lost my virginity to him.

At first, I laughed it off, naively thinking that since everyone knew how much James and I hated each other, no one would ever believe it. But they did. Every single person believed James, and after that lie, no guy asked me out or even looked at me in passing. It was devastating to a sixteen-year-old girl to have that kind of stuff being said about her.

It was even worse when I confronted James about it, demanding he take back the lie and tell people the truth.

He smirked at me before telling me, "No," like that was the end of the conversation.

But, apparently, it was because I had been too mortified to bring it up again, and he had been too satisfied with himself over ruining my reputation to ever take it back.

It was a funny thing—a girl's word versus a guy's. Why was it that no one ever believed the girl when sex was involved?

DRUNK CONFESSIONS

James

LOOKING AT JULIA La Bella was like staring at the sun. I couldn't look for too long or else it started to really fucking hurt. Yeah, I knew that was a cheesy-as-hell comparison, but the woman was a goddess. She always had been.

I'd learned the definition of beautiful the first time I ever laid eyes on her as a little kid. A part of me fell in love with her then even though she hated my guts and couldn't stand being anywhere near me. I didn't blame her though. The second we found out about each other, we were raised to despise the other. I'd just never been any good at following the rules, especially ones that made no fucking sense.

I was pretty sure that if Julia could get away with murdering me, she'd at least give it the old college try. The death stare she currently penetrated me with only furthered my feelings on the matter. Her best friend, Jeanine, however, would definitely try and stop her though. I wasn't sure what the hell I'd ever done to get on Jeanine's good side, but I'd always be thankful for it.

"I really need to get to work here, ladies. I'm sure you need to do the same." I flashed a charming smile at the group of women who had gathered around my booth and refused to leave.

No matter how disinterested I appeared, they didn't give up or go away. They were relentless in their pursuits. And trust me; I recognized the irony that was my life.

"See you after the competition," they all threatened before scattering back to where they belonged.

I cast another glance over at Julia, and my damn breath caught in my throat. She had always affected me that way, and there was a pretty good chance that she always would. Which, let's be honest, didn't fare well for my future relationships if she wasn't a part of it.

Being raised to not only hate, but also stay the hell away from the one girl who starred in every single teenage fantasy had been the bane of my existence. Do you have any idea how hard it is to "stay away" from the girl next door?

I mean, literally.

My property line ends where hers begins. Acres of vines divide the La Bella winery from the Russos' but not our homes. You would think that with all that expansive land, our great-grandfathers would have built the main houses to have some seclusion and privacy, but no, the idiots had practically built them right on top of each other.

And the worst part? I had grown up being able to see Julia's bedroom window from mine. Talk about some piss-poor parental planning. How the hell was I ever supposed to fall out of love with the girl if she never left my line of sight? And then there were nights where I swore she'd left her curtains open on purpose, just so I could see her getting undressed for bed. She tortured me in every possible way, but she never gave in, never crossed the invisible line separating us even though, at the time, I would have bet my life that she wanted to just as badly as I did.

That was why I started inviting girls over and making sure that Julia would see them up in my room with me. I freaked out one night after catching her staring from her window to mine. It was exactly what I had wanted, but she actually looked hurt. I thought about her doing the exact same thing to me in retaliation, and I would have deserved it, but the idea of seeing Julia with some arrogant loser from our high school grated on my every nerve. My insides twisted in a jealous rage at the mere thought of another guy's hands touching any part of her skin or being in places that I was forbidden from ever entering. I'd stopped bringing girls home that night.

"Are you going to sit there, daydreaming all day, or are we going to pour this wine?" My best friend, Dane, appeared out of thin air and clapped me on the back.

I had no idea how long he'd been standing there, watching me watch her.

"I wasn't daydreaming," I bit out and reached for a bottle a little too aggressively, spilling some of the contents out of the top.

"Reminiscing, daydreaming, fantasizing"—he shrugged as he wiped up my mess, his too-long blond hair falling over his eyes—"whatever you want to call it."

I could have continued to lie to him, but it was pointless. Dane was the only one who knew how I felt about Julia.

"I was just thinking back."

"So, you *were* reminiscing," he said in a know-it-all tone. "What part are we reliving this time?" Sometimes, my best friend was a real asshole. "Ooh, I know." He raised his hand like he was waiting for me to call on him. "Drunk confessions in the vineyard. You know that's my favorite."

My temper started to flare. "Of course the single most humiliating and heartbreaking night of my life would be your favorite. How are we even friends?"

"For the record, I was being sarcastic," he said the words ridiculously slow like I was some sort of knuckle-dragging caveman who couldn't comprehend them. "And I only mentioned that particular moment in time because I know it's the one you enjoy torturing yourself with the most. You're nothing if not self-deprecating when it comes to that woman."

He wasn't wrong. I had been working up to that particular scene before he interrupted me with his presence.

"I just need the reminder sometimes."

"The reminder that she fake hates you?"

"The reminder that she really does." I winced.

"You and I both know that's bullshit. You could put yourself out there and just tell her how you feel," he offered with a shrug.

"I'm never doing that again," I said a little too bitterly, but the memory still felt fresh.

"Come on, James. That night was so long ago, and she was drunk. You're both adults now. Or at least, you pretend to be."

"It's not a good idea," I said around the lump in my throat when all I could really wonder was, *What if she rejects me again?*

The scene played out in my head without warning.

A DOOR SLAMMED in the distance, and I looked out my window to see Julia stalking off toward her vineyard with multiple bottles of wine in her arms.

What the hell is she doing? *I wondered.*

I watched her, focusing on her every move, her every step. Before she ducked into a row of lush vines, she turned around and looked directly into my bedroom window. Our eyes locked, and she paused for what felt like an eternity before she turned and disappeared from view.

Was that intentional, or did I surprise her by watching? Was that an invitation of sorts for me to follow her? What did it mean? What did she want?

I had no idea, but I sat in my room, trying to figure it out for too long before I sucked it up and decided to go find her. Tonight would be the night that I finally confessed to Julia La Bella that I had feelings for her, our parents be damned.

Sneaking out of my house was easy, but trying to find Julia was a pain in the ass. I wasn't familiar with her property at all, so attempting to navigate it made me feel like I was a blind mouse in a maze.

"What do you want, Russo?" Her voice carried over the grapes and led me straight to her. She had four separate bottles of wine propped next to her, and she was apparently drinking them all.

"What are you doing?"

She shrugged her shoulders. "I figured, if I was going to run this place someday, I might as well try to like the stuff." She sipped from her glass and wrinkled her nose. "It's so gross. How do people drink this?"

I laughed because I had the same reaction each time I was forced to try our wine as well. "I've heard it's an acquired taste," I said as I sat across from her.

"That's what they say about beer, too. I don't know about you, but if something has to be an 'acquired taste,'" she said with air quotes, "I think that means it sucks."

"How much have you had to drink?"

"Why do you care?" she snapped, and I knew she was at least buzzed.

"I care because …" I paused, almost too nervous to answer honestly.

She took another gulp of the wine and winced, waving her hand for me to continue. "Because what?"

Shit. Here goes everything, *I thought to myself before word-vomiting all over her.*

"Because I like you. I've always liked you, Julia. Since the moment I first saw you," I said, a little too honest for my own good.

"When we were four. I remember. But what are you even saying right now? Do you hear yourself?" Her tone sounded almost offended, which made no sense.

"Of course I hear myself." I scooted closer in the dirt, so I could touch her if she let me. "I'm telling you that I like you."

I reached for the hand resting on her knee, but she pulled it away.

"You don't like me, Russo. You like a challenge. You like the things you think you can't have."

"Seriously?" It was my turn to feel offended.

The look in her eyes practically leveled me. "Seriously. You don't like anything that comes too easily. You never have. That's probably why you think you like me, but you don't really."

"You don't get to tell me how I feel about you."

"Whatever. I'm sure this is some sort of game. Did Dane put you up to this? Did you make some kind of bet with your stupid basketball team?" She started to hiccup, but it didn't stop her. "Why don't you go spend time with one of the many girls I've seen in your room lately?"

"Julia, look at me," I pleaded, and her glazed-over eyes met mine. I shouldn't be doing this while she was drunk, but it was now or never. "I have feelings for you. I wish they would go the fuck away, but they won't. They never have. And they never will."

She started laughing and couldn't stop. It got uncomfortable, and right before I pushed to my feet, she said, "Feelings? Do you even know what feelings are? I'm sure you don't. I hate you, Russo. I want nothing to do with you. And I never will."

"You really feel that way? You, Julia La Bella, genuinely hate me and not just because our parents have told us to for our whole lives?" My heart felt like a boulder inside my chest, suddenly too heavy, too burdensome, as I waited for her answer.

"Not because of our parents. I really feel that way." She swallowed hard but avoided all eye contact with me.

"You've never once thought about what it would be like to be together?"

"Why on earth would I ever think about being with you?"

Without responding to her question, I left. I believed her when she said that she hated me. And I believed when she said she wanted nothing to do with me. But I couldn't handle it. I'd worn my heart on my sleeve, and she'd ripped it off, thrown it on the ground, and stomped all over it without a second thought. The rejection stung. More than that, it fucking ached. Each beat of my heart reminded me that she didn't want me; she would never want me, and I was a fool for ever thinking she could.

Why the hell did I put myself out there like that?

I swore I'd never do it again. Not for Julia La Bella and not for any girl.

DANE SNAPPED HIS fingers in front of my face, and I shook my head.

"Yeah, yeah. What?"

"Drunk confessions?" he asked a little too smugly, already knowing the answer.

"Maybe."

I had no idea how to get Julia to stop hating me, to stop judging me for something I had no part in. I hadn't even been born when our great-grandfathers made that stupid bet that ruined our families' lives. I had nothing to do with it, and neither did she. Yet she despised me as if I'd burned down her vineyards with my own two hands.

The most ironic part of this whole thing was that it was her damn family who had won the bet in the first place. So, if anyone should hate anyone, it should be me hating her. I had every right. Instead, all I could think about was getting my hands underneath that tight-as-hell skirt she currently wore and plunging my fingers inside her. I'd dreamed about the way Julia La Bella would feel underneath my touch for too many years. I'd salivated, just thinking about the way she must taste. I'd bet it was as sweet as the wine she made.

"You've had it bad for her since we were five years old."

"Four," I corrected. If the motherfucker was going to start spouting off ages, it was at least going to be the right one.

"What?" He looked at me, confused.

"I've had it bad for her since I was four. My birthday party, remember? It was the first time I ever saw her," I explained like he hadn't been standing next to me that day.

Our respective families had apparently done their damnedest to keep us apart since birth. I had no idea how we'd never seen each other before that day, but up until then, I had no clue there were any other kids around for miles. Someone must have gotten sloppy on my fourth birthday because Julia came running out of her house with a bright pink dress on, her hair in two pigtails, as she waved at me like we were long-lost friends before her father wrapped his arms around her waist and pulled her back inside the house, kicking and screaming.

Our lives crossed that morning, and they'd yet to come undone.

"Yeah, you asked me if I could see the angel, too, or if only you could see her," Dane repeated the story that was seared in my brain.

I let out a soft laugh. "And you said you didn't see any angel, but you saw some dumb girl."

Dane shrugged. "I think, between the two of us, my assessment was more right. Julia La Bella is no angel."

My gaze swung to him, narrowing. "Watch it," I warned.

His hands raised in the air in defeat. "Don't shoot the messenger. I'm just saying, she's no angel, is all." He picked up a glass of wine and downed it in one gulp instead of sipping it like you were supposed to do. "This is good stuff." He twirled the glass between his fingers before refilling it and downing it a second time. "It's really fucking good."

"I know."

"Think it will beat hers?" He gave a head nod in Julia's direction.

I swallowed hard as I looked at her for what had to be the thousandth time already. I blew out a quick breath, forcing my eyes away from her body. "Probably not."

"Will you ever stop trying?" He gave me the side-eye, and I had no idea if he was being serious or not.

The winery was in my blood. I'd been groomed to take it over, to create and make wine from our vines. As much as I hated losing year after year, quitting wasn't an option.

"Why would I stop trying?"

"No reason. Just asking, is all." He started to turn his back to me, and I placed a strong grip on his shoulder.

"No, really. Why would I stop competing? This is my livelihood. My business. My career. Why would I ever stop doing what I love?" My blood pressure started rising as my pulse quickened. It took all of two seconds to get me completely defensive.

"James, I was just asking." He pulled my hand from his shoulder. "You don't have to compete year after year in order to have a successful winery, and we both know it. These competitions are just an added bonus, a feather in your cap really, a little extra publicity that you don't even need. You're already running one of the most lucrative wineries in the state, with or without this shit." He waved a hand around the crowded space.

He wasn't wrong. I didn't have to do these sorts of things. But I wanted to. It was the only way I got close to her. I knew exactly why I kept entering every single one of them, and Dane did, too. If I didn't, then I'd never see Julia La Bella in this capacity. Especially not since she had moved out of the main house and had a separate bungalow built where I could no longer see her from any window on my property. I always suspected she'd done that on purpose.

"Should I go try the she-devil's wine? See what we're working against?" he suggested with a sly grin, and my skin prickled.

"You know better than to call her that," I said between clenched teeth.

The first time he'd called Julia a she-devil, she'd overheard him and started to cry. I punched him right in the stomach because of it. Our third grade teacher forced him to apologize in front of the entire classroom, and I had to apologize as well. I had done it, but my fingers had been crossed behind my back because I wasn't sorry. I wasn't sorry at all.

"Anyone ever told you that you're delusional?" he asked, shaking his head in disbelief.

"Just you," I said in response because Dane was the only one I'd ever willingly admitted anything to.

From the outside looking in, I hated Julia the same way she hated me. I acted cocky, arrogant, and sometimes a little mean. It was my defense mechanism; bad attention was still attention, right?

"You can't keep doing this to yourself, man."

"Doing what exactly?"

"Waiting," he said, diagnosing me like some sort of love expert.

I raised my brows and cocked my head. "I'm not waiting. I've had two serious relationships in the last two years. I'm just taking a break from women right now until the right one comes along. Women are exhausting."

He lowered the bottle of wine he was holding to the table before clasping his hands together in prayer pose. "Okay. I'm going there. Neither one of those relationships was 'serious.'" His hands unclasped as he did finger quotes in the air.

"How was Rebecca not serious? We were together for a year," I argued.

"Seattle Rebecca was a joke. You never saw her. It only lasted that long because she kept thinking you'd change. Once she realized you never would, she bowed out. And, ever since her, you've been burying yourself in the winery, pretending to be overworked, but I know it's because you're waiting for her. Waiting for what exactly, I have no idea. But you're still waiting. And it's painful to watch, man."

When had my idiot best friend become so observant?

I exhaled as all of my thoughts and emotions warred against each other. "I think a part of me has always assumed she'll stop with the hate and admit what we've always known."

"Which is what exactly?"

"That there's something between us. I know it. She knows it. It's undeniable."

I held my breath as I waited for that day to come. I was clearly still holding it.

"It is. Everyone can see it. But you should really tell her how you feel," he urged. "Before someone else goes after her and you lose your chance." He gave a nod toward Todd Lestare, current marketing director of Lestare Winery and my former basketball teammate in high school.

Jealousy reared her ugly head with a vengeance. I never trusted Todd when it came to Julia and for good reason. He always lingered around her booth a little too long, always staring at her a little too hard. Not to mention the fact that he'd wanted Julia since high school, and I'd made him walk away from her then. There was no way that I had that kind of control now that we were grown men. I hated watching him with her—the way he made her laugh, the way he touched her arm like he had every right to it. If I lost Julia to him, of all people, I'd never forgive myself.

Sucking in a long breath, I nodded to myself before focusing on Dane, a newfound confidence coursing through my veins. "I think you might be right."

Dane's body language suddenly changed, and his face turned completely animated. "Really? You'll tell her? You'll actually tell her?"

"If I don't, someone else is going to, and it's going to destroy me to sit back and watch, knowing I did nothing to stop it."

His eyes widened. "Okay. So, Operation Julia is officially back on?"

I laughed at the name we'd come up with in the seventh grade after we convinced ourselves that we could get Julia to kiss me before school let out for the summer. We'd failed, and the operation had been canceled—or at least, paused indefinitely.

"Looks that way. And, this time, it's going to work."

Dane didn't look convinced. "Wanna bet on it?"

"Do you?" I countered.

"Betting doesn't end well in your family," he said as he gripped my hand and shook it hard, "so I'd be a fool not to."

FIRST PLACE

Julia

FIVE HOURS OF schmoozing, people-pleasing, and smiling were finally nearing an end. It wasn't that I didn't love this part of my job, but I was exhausted. Being forced to be *on* in that way took a lot out of a person. It sounded stupid, I knew that, but it didn't make it any less true.

"How are you holding up?" Jeanine whispered as the last few glasses of our wine disappeared.

I smiled at her before answering, "Good. Tired."

"I know. This shit's exhausting." She shook her head and rubbed at the back of her neck. "And I don't even do half the entertaining that you do."

"All part of the job." I faked a curtsy and wished like hell I could take off my heels. As soon as the winner was announced, I'd slip them off and tuck them into my bag.

"Todd Lestare is going to ask you out again. I overheard some girls talking in the restroom about him and James."

I groaned and rolled my eyes. Todd wasn't my type, not even in high school, but he never seemed to take no for an answer. To be fair, every time he asked me out and I turned him down, my reasons were flimsy, my excuses weak. I told him things like I had too much going on at the winery to get away or it was harvest season or I was in the middle of a launch or rebrand. Instead of figuring out that I wasn't interested in him, he took my rejections as temporary setbacks. I should be honest and straightforward, but I had no idea how to do that without hurting his feelings and feeling like a jerk in return. The only person whose feelings I never cared about hurting was James. I thought I got a sick joy out of being mean to him. I decided to psychoanalyze that part of myself later.

"You could do me a solid and take him off my hands, you know." I nudged Jeanine with my shoulder.

"I would, but I like to date guys who are actually interested in me and not my best friend." She threw her hands up in surrender. "Unfortunately, that narrows down my choices."

"So selfish." I shook my head in mock disappointment.

"I know." She played along. "It's a super-rude requirement of mine."

We both laughed.

It wasn't that there was anything really wrong with Todd. I just felt nothing for him. There was no attraction or chemistry. He was a good-looking guy, if you were into blond hair and the clean-cut type, which I wasn't.

I cast a quick glance over toward James, who was staring at me, and my heart jumped into my throat before I looked away just as quickly. Apparently, I was into the more forbidden type with dark hair and a perfectly trimmed beard. The kind of guy who made my heart feel like it was going to break out of my chest with just a look.

My inner bad girl liked guys who could ruin my life and make my parents disown me with just one kiss.

"They're about to announce the winners," Jeanine said.

We both focused our attention toward the stage as the mic clicked on, and the speakers crackled to life. Nerves flooded my entire body as I waited for them to read through their long-winded script and get to the good stuff.

"And the winner of this year's Limited Production Wine is"—the announcer sucked in a long, deep breath and paused for what felt like half an hour—"La Bella with their fantastic Chianti cinnamon blend. Honorable mention goes to Russo Wines with their delicious orange-flavored cab. We hope you had a chance to try both of them this afternoon. Congratulations."

The tiredness I'd felt only moments ago immediately disappeared as energy zipped in to replace it. A huge smile spread across my face that I couldn't wipe away if I tried. But then again, why would I? Winning wasn't something I took for granted or assumed would be handed to me even though it might have looked that way from the outside. I'd worked hard to create this blend, just like I had every year, but I had to admit that I was getting sort of used to coming in first place.

What would happen when the time came and I eventually lost out to someone? And what if I lost to James?

Shuddering at the thought, I shook my head, refusing to think about that sort of thing as people swarmed the booth and doled out their congratulations. I gracefully accepted them all, and when I was presented with the award-winning medal, blue ribbon, official certificate, and emblem, I found myself anxious.

Most wineries had a sticker printed up that they either slapped onto the bottle or had them incorporated into the original label for their award-winning wine. But not La Bella. I had the emblem forged into a metal stamp that I would dip into hot wax and hand-stamp onto each bottle. Each of our award winners had a different emblem and color near the neck. This year's would be dark blue. To be honest, I was running out of color options.

"You did it." Jeanine pulled me toward her and squeezed me. "Never a doubt in my mind."

"That makes one of us," I said, the grin still firmly plastered across my face as I removed my painful heels and stepped into a pair of well-worn UGG boots. They didn't go with my outfit in the slightest, but my screaming feet thanked me the moment the fur surrounded them. My personal comfort was far more important at this point in the day than looking the part.

"Congratulations"—James appeared in front of my booth as I set about dismantling it—"again."

My smile faltered. "Thanks," I said without looking up. The last thing I wanted to do was give James a reason to hang around longer.

"Don't you get tired of winning?"

Standing straight up, I leveled him with my gaze. "Don't you get tired of losing?"

"Not particularly," he answered with a shrug, and I wondered what his angle was.

"Ugh, Russo, what do you want?" I feigned annoyance at Mr. Honorable Mention.

"I want to take you out to dinner to celebrate," he said, sounding so sincere that I almost believed that he had no ulterior motive.

"Yeah, right. You probably want to steal my grapes."

"How the hell would I steal your grapes?" He looked at me like I was half-crazy.

I waved a hand in the air. "I don't know. Distract me with dinner while your minions pull my vines out of the ground? I have no idea."

"The only thing I ever wanted to steal from you was your virginity," he whispered as he leaned toward me.

I couldn't tell if he was joking or not. "Ha-ha. Very funny. You already told everyone that you did that back in high school. Thanks for that by the way. Such a gentleman."

A surprised sound escaped his lips. "You really don't know, do you?"

"Know what?" I propped my hip out and rested my hand there.

"Come with me to dinner, and I'll tell you."

He flashed a grin that was so damn charming that I was sure it worked on every female he'd ever given it to. It was definitely starting to work on me. I glanced over at Jeanine for help, but she pretended not to be listening.

"Jeanine can come, too," he added.

Oh, James Russo was good.

"What? Me?" Jeanine started to stutter on her response. "I can't go with you two. I, uh … have plans."

"You do not!" I practically shouted because I knew for a fact that she had absolutely zero plans.

"Well, I still can't go. Leave me out of whatever this is." She gave us both a quick frown before disappearing to God knows where.

"Great. You scared my best friend away."

I disapprovingly shook my head before James took a step toward me, closing the space between us. My body should have moved away from his in response, but it stayed deathly still, enjoying the cat-and-mouse game we played. Desire sprang to life inside me even though it knew it didn't stand a chance. Giving in to James wasn't something I could do, but I was tempted. The smell of his cologne surrounded me, and it took everything in me to not close my eyes and breathe it in. I wanted him even closer, and I practically dared him to make the small distance between us evaporate. I hated how attracted I was to him; it made me weak.

"Dinner, Julia. Say yes. I won't stop asking."

"No," I managed to get out.

A quick guffaw escaped his lips. "Yes."

"No," I said once more, but if he asked again, I was definitely going to cave.

"Julia, say yes."

My mouth opened to do exactly that when Todd Lestare interrupted us, "Are you almost ready to go, Julia?"

I stared at him in shock, my mouth still open.

"Um, almost," I stumbled over the lie.

James's expression turned downright murderous. "What is this?" He turned his head and focused on Todd, his jaw tense.

I couldn't remember a time I'd ever seen him look so angry. *Why was he so mad?*

"I'm taking Julia to dinner to celebrate her win. She finally said yes. Only had to ask about ten times." Todd winked, and I died a little inside. Getting me out of going to dinner with James was one thing, but piling more lies on top was more than I needed or wanted.

"Is that so?" James looked fiercely into my eyes and waited for me to come clean. He knew I was lying. He dared me to admit it, to say it out loud, but I couldn't.

I offered him a weak nod instead.

He leaned in close, his lips nearing my ear. "Don't go out with him," he whispered, and I had to catch my breath. "Anyone but him."

My mouth opened to respond, to tell him that I'd do whatever the heck he asked, but Todd stepped in again.

"Not sure what game you're playing at, Russo, but we've got reservations to make. And I know that you, of all people, can understand that."

It was a low blow, but it worked. James had made quite the reputation for himself in our small town. If you made a private tasting reservation and didn't show up or cancel with him in advance, he wouldn't let you make another reservation again. Ever. And it didn't matter who you were, what family you belonged to, or how famous you might be. I used to think that made him more of an arrogant jerk, but once it started happening to me during tourist season, too, I understood his reasoning.

James stalked away, mumbling profanities, looking more pissed off than ever.

I turned toward Todd. "Thanks for the save, but you didn't have to say that to him."

"I knew it would piss him off." Todd sounded smug, and it made me want to punch him in the face for being so cruel.

Once again, I was clearly the only one who was allowed to mistreat James.

"It was still unnecessary."

I started to finish packing up, assuming that Todd would walk away and do the same.

"I meant it, you know," he said, and I turned to find that he hadn't moved an inch.

"Meant what?" I wasn't sure if he was referring to the dinner or the stuff about James.

"Dinner. Come on. You can't avoid me forever."

"Oh, I don't think that's a good idea." I started to get uncomfortable as I searched my brain for excuses that he would buy.

"Give me one good reason why not."

"Uh, because we're friends," I offered even though we technically weren't friends. Acquaintances was more like it.

"Friends eat dinner together," he said with a lopsided grin.

"Friends do. But I'm not sure that's really your angle," I said directly, hoping to dissuade him.

"Well"—he paused—"friends who become more than friends start with dinner."

"Todd"—I sucked in a quick breath—"I'm not looking to date anyone right now. I don't want any complications or distractions. And I don't see that changing anytime soon. My focus is on the winery, and that's all I have time for."

The truth was that if I were genuinely interested in Todd, I would have served him up a different speech altogether, one that included me saying yes, and I would have fit him into my life at the winery the way I had with the few guys I briefly dated in the past. But I wasn't interested in Todd. And I never would be.

He laughed out loud, and I had no idea what was even so funny.

"It's just dinner, Julia. Come on. What could possibly go wrong?"

Famous last words, I thought to myself before reluctantly agreeing to go strictly as friends.

My skin prickled with the thought that I should know better. I should know that absolutely everything could go wrong. And would.

JEALOUSY FUELS THE FIRE

James

"MOTHERFUCKER." I KICKED an empty box and watched it fly across the room, narrowly missing hitting someone in the back.

"What the hell happened?" Dane asked, his brow furrowed.

"Todd Lestare happened."

"What does that even mean?"

I rubbed at my eyes with the palms of my hands, willing the image of Todd and Julia to erase itself, but it was no use. Too pissed off to explain this to my best friend, I simply filled him in. "She's apparently going to dinner with *him*," I practically growled.

His expression soured. "How did that happen?"

"I guess he asked her first. I don't know."

"So, you what, walked away? And left Todd LeDouche alone with her?" he asked between bouts of laughter. "I never knew you were such a quitter."

I was already angry enough; I didn't need Dane adding to it with the name-calling and his inane laughter. "Quitter? Maybe it's not meant to be. Maybe God stepped in to stop me from getting my heart crushed for a second time by the same woman. You ever think of that?"

"No," he answered sternly. "You ever think that maybe God sent Todd LeDouche to step in to see how hard you'd fight to get the girl?"

"No," I responded just as sternly as he had. "He asked her out. She said yes." My teeth were unknowingly grinding together, and I only stopped once Dane gave me a little slap on the shoulder, forcing me to catch my breath and slow my heart rate.

"I can see you're totally fine with it. No way in hell she's interested in Lestare," Dane said, but I was only half-listening. "We'll follow them. Eat where they eat. Go where they go. We'll make that date uncomfortable as hell. We'll be the unwanted third and fourth wheels."

Surprisingly, I actually considered his stupid plan for all of five seconds before bowing out. "No. I'm going to cut my losses and lick my wounds from the comfort of my own home. I'm exhausted anyway."

He knew better than to argue, but that usually never stopped him.

"Really? Home instead of ruining their night? You sure?"

I nodded. "I'm sure."

"All right. I'll give you until we leave this place to change your mind"—he tossed me a sympathetic look—"but I get it if you don't."

I wasn't going to change my mind. I felt like a big enough idiot already tonight, and I had no interest in humiliating myself more.

Stepping into the night air, I noticed how unseasonably warm it still was outside. There was very little wind, but damn it if it wasn't the perfect night for a date. Blowing out a long breath, I unlocked my car door and sat inside. I needed to paint, and I couldn't get home quick enough to start.

Only three people in the world knew that I painted—my mother, my father, and Dane. Other than that, I kept it to myself even though the walls of my room and our home were covered with my artistic creations. I painted our winery, the buildings, the vines, the town, Julia's vineyard, and even some label mockups for our special-edition wines, but so far, I hadn't been able to convince my parents to ditch the traditional logo and try one of mine. They were so rooted in tradition and what worked that they were afraid to rock the boat.

Pulling my car into the driveway, I hopped out and headed straight toward the small barn where my paints and canvas were set up. Some people wrote out their frustrations with words in journals or books but not me. I'd never been good with writing, and when Julia had basically stepped on my heart that night in the vineyard back in high school, I'd come here and painted until the sun rose. She said I had no feelings, but I spilled them all over seven canvases that night, painting broken hearts on fire with vines twisting through them and a shattered heart among the rubble as she walked away from it. I painted out my pain, and by morning, even though I was exhausted, I thought I felt better. That was, until I had seen her at school, and she'd refused to even acknowledge my existence.

Dipping my brush into the red acrylic paint, I swiped it across the stark white canvas in long brushstrokes, my heart screaming in anger as thoughts of Julia with Todd filled my head. It was the smell that pulled me out first. I stopped moving as I breathed in the air, my skin suddenly alive with the awareness that something was wrong. I knew that scent all too well.

Throwing open the barn door, I ran outside. The smell of fire was definitely stronger, and I could see the smoke and the light of the flames rising through the darkness in the distance.

"Dad!" I screamed as I pulled out my phone and dialed 911. "Dad!" I yelled again as I started sprinting.

Running for the back of our property in the dark toward the light of the flames, I slammed to an abrupt halt when I saw the actual fire, my eyes practically bulging out of my head at how close it was and how high the orange bursts were shooting into the night's sky. I said a quick thank you to whoever listened for the lack of wind and prayed the air would stay still.

"Nine-one-one. What's your emergency?"

"Tina, it's James Russo," I stuttered, recognizing the voice of the operator. "There's a fire on the land behind mine and the La Bellas'. Send the trucks quickly. It's growing and heading straight for the property."

"Stay on the line with me, James," she started to say.

But I yelled at her to hurry up and send the trucks before ending the call. I couldn't stay on the phone with her and try to stop these flames from reaching our property at the same time.

Where the hell is my dad? I wondered before hearing him shout from somewhere behind me.

"I'm out here, Dad," I yelled back, knowing he couldn't see me in the dark. "Turn on the sprinkler systems. Keep the water running," I yelled as I doubled back. I grabbed one of our power hoses and sprinted toward the edge of our property line.

The fire started to creep perilously close to Julia's famous south side vines, which were way less protected than the rest of the vineyards. While most vines were consistently moist and offered a natural barrier against fire, I knew that her south side ones tended to be drier because of their placement on the hill. They were also surrounded by brush that couldn't be easily cleared, unlike a normal vineyard with perfectly spaced out and meticulously maintained grounds. The fire would eat her prized vines first and think nothing of it. My heart ached as I thought about Julia losing the thing she loved most.

"What are you doing?" my father practically screamed from behind me as I turned away from our property line and toward the La Bellas'.

With the water set on high, I worked to protect Julia's vines on the cliff, creating a barrier around them the best I could without falling off the damn thing. Climbing down as far as I could go while maintaining my balance, I sprayed and pounded at the oncoming flames, determined to keep them at bay and praying I didn't fall. I slipped constantly, my feet trying to brace and dig in as the fire cracked and roared through the brush, eating every single thing in its path, making it clear that we were at war, the fire and me.

The sounds of sirens in the distance only gave me marginal relief as I sprayed and moved the best I could. I swore I heard the fire laugh at me as it jumped and lurched toward the cliff-side vines before backing down and then roaring back up again with a vengeance. The firemen couldn't get here quick enough.

"James!" The sound of my father's angry voice hit my ears, and I glanced back for only a second.

The sprinklers were raining down on our vines, but Julia's weren't on. *Where the hell were her parents?*

Imagining the look on her face if she lost the vineyard was almost enough to break me in two. I couldn't let it happen. I wouldn't. The flames doubled in size, creating its own weather, making wind from within itself as if it needed little else to help fuel it. I continued to spray at it from every direction, moving my body in angles that fucking ached as I held the weight of the hose in my arms. I realized in that moment that there was no way I was going to win this battle, but I refused to quit.

The sirens grew louder, and I knew they were here, but I was afraid to stop fighting and look back to check.

"James, we'll take it from here." A handful of firemen suddenly fanned out around me, gallons of water spraying out from all directions as the vineyard lit up. "We got this. Get back," one of them said, but I was afraid to stop. "James! Get out of here," he shouted, and I finally dropped my hose and took a breath, my arms shaking.

The flames were already starting to back down with the amount of pressure and power they wielded against it at once. It could have been so much worse. Fires had the ability to destroy entire towns without a second thought, and they had burned half of this one once in the past.

I started to walk away, feeling a little dazed.

"James."

Julia came to a running stop in front of me, and I stopped walking, too. Whatever existed between us zinged to life, and there was no way she didn't feel it, too. Her hands reached for my shoulders, and I couldn't remember the last time she'd physically touched me.

"Are you okay? What are you doing all the way out here? Are you hurt?" She swiped her thumb across my forehead, and I winced. "You're bleeding."

"I am?" I wiped at my head and noticed the blood on my fingertips. I had no idea how that had even happened.

"What happened?" She reached inside her purse and pulled something out, pressing it against my head.

I let her take care of me—not only because she was offering for the first time in our lives, but also because I wanted her to.

"I don't know, but I tried, Julia. I'm so sorry," I told her, wanting so badly to hug her and never let go.

"Sorry for what?" she asked. Her eyes were on mine, filled with concern for what I believed was me and not her vines.

"I tried to save your vines," I said.

A surprised gasp escaped her lips as she looked over my shoulder and took three leaping steps past me, as if only now realizing that they had been in danger.

She walked back to me, her face pinched. "You tried to save *my* vines?" she asked, repeating my words.

I nodded, feeling exhausted and defeated as the adrenaline started to filter out. "I tried, but the flames were so close. And they wouldn't stop."

"James …" She reached for my hand and clasped her fingers with mine. It was such an intimate gesture, but it wasn't something that we did. Julia La Bella was never supposed to hold my hand. "They didn't burn."

"They didn't?"

"No. Come look." She pulled me to the edge of the cliff and pointed.

Where the fire had once been very much alive and breathing, nothing but smoke and small hot spots remained.

Relief flooded through me. "They're okay," I breathed out, tangling my free hand in my hair.

She smiled, nodding. "Because of you. Why'd you do that?" she asked before dropping my hand like it could no longer be trusted.

"Do what?" My brain was spinning with confusion, with exhaustion, with a thousand emotions hitting me all at once.

"Why did you save my vines instead of your own? Your dad's going to kill you."

In that moment, I had forgotten that anyone else existed, especially my dad. Glancing away from the charred remains of the fire, I looked hard into Julia's hazel eyes. "I know how much they mean to you. It would have killed you to lose them."

"So? What do you care if I lose them or not?" she asked sincerely. Julia was genuinely confused.

I considered telling her that I was in love with her, always had been. I wanted to lay it all out on the line, but something stopped me. "I don't like seeing you hurt," was all I could admit.

Her expression instantly softened. "That's funny. Are you joking?"

"What's funny?"

"It's just that I would have thought the exact opposite, is all."

I swallowed hard, her words stinging. "You think I like seeing you hurt?"

She shrugged slowly, her shoulders scrunching up at the same time as her lip curled. "I just didn't think you cared either way, to be honest. You didn't care in high school, so why would you care now?"

She was talking about the rumor I'd started back then. Hell, if it wasn't our parents coming between us, my mistake sure was.

"I've always cared."

Her hips moved as she shifted her weight from foot to foot. "Okay. Well, thank you." She tilted her head. "This isn't a trick, right?"

"How would this be a trick?"

"I don't know," she stuttered, clearly rattled for whatever reason.

Had I really been that big of an asshole to her that she would question a good deed and think there was malicious intent behind it?

"I just don't understand why you would do this for my family. My dad is going to flip out when I tell him."

"What do you mean? Like he's going to be pissed?" Those words were the last thing I'd expected to hear.

Her eyes pulled together as she contemplated how to explain her thoughts to me. "My dad's going to feel like he owes you. And he's not going to be able to stand it. This will probably make him hate you more." She actually sounded annoyed, and that little crack in her armor gave me hope. "It's so stupid. It should make him hate you less, right? But I know it won't."

She took a few steps toward me before cupping my chin with her hand and pressing a quick kiss against my cheek. All the blood rushed to my pants, and I wanted to turn my head and change this G-rated kiss into something more suited for adults.

"Thank you again. I can never repay you for what you've done," she said before backing away and putting distance between us.

I wondered if she regretted what she'd just done, but I sure as shit wasn't going to ask and give her a chance to tell me yes.

"Where are your parents, by the way? I'm surprised your dad wasn't out here, trying to push me into the fire."

She actually laughed, and I wanted to bottle that sound up and listen to it on repeat whenever I was having a shit day.

"They're in Italy, visiting family."

"Go out with me," I said, refusing to take no for an answer this time.

"Go out with you?" she repeated.

"You do that a lot."

"Do what?"

"Repeat the things I say."

"I do?"

"James! Get the hell over here." My dad sounded absolutely pissed.

I was honestly surprised he'd let me talk to Julia for this long without interrupting. I wondered briefly how much he'd seen.

"That's how you can thank me for saving the vines. Go out with me." I started to back away, hoping she'd say yes.

She kicked the dirt with her feet, her arms wrapped around her middle. "I knew this was a trick."

I laughed. "Julia, one date won't kill you."

"One date with you might," she fired back, and I hated how much her attitude turned me on.

"So, that's a yes?" I stopped walking and waited.

My dad screamed my name again, and I suddenly felt like I was a teenager about to get grounded for doing something wrong.

"I'm not taking no for an answer, so you might as well give in."

"Fine. But I won't enjoy myself." Julia waved me off before turning her back to me.

I sprinted toward my still-standing house, thankful that the fire hadn't gotten out of control and burned it all to the ground, as I mentally planned to make sure that Julia not only enjoyed herself, but also never wanted the night to end.

There would be no more denying what had always existed between us. The mutual charade would end on our date. I'd make sure of it, our parents be damned.

IT'S ABOUT DAMN TIME

Julia

I ONLY PRETENDED to walk back to my place to encourage James to leave and deal with his dad, but in reality, I stayed outside to talk to the firemen. They told me that if it hadn't been for James, the fire definitely would have spread, most likely reaching both of our wine barns and homes, and it might have become an unstoppable force. They also told me that they had practically had to physically remove him from the cliff because he wouldn't stop battling the flames on his own.

I listened to their every word in shock. James really had been some kind of hero, and I still couldn't understand why. Fighting for his own vineyard was one thing, but he had fought for mine and left his unattended. I couldn't wrap my head around it. It was hard to reconcile the kind of guy I had always assumed James was with the one I'd witnessed last night. All that cocky, arrogant facade had shifted into something that seemed actually human and caring. It threw me for a loop. Not that I didn't enjoy seeing James that way—because I did—but it made my heart do funny things inside my chest. I wasn't sure how I felt about that.

My parents had heard about the fire from someone in town, but I had no idea who. They called me at four in the morning and insisted that they get on the next flight and come home. I calmed them down and convinced them to stay in Italy for the remainder of their trip, but I knew the worst was yet to come. Once my dad found out about what James had done, he was going to lose his ever-loving mind. If it was up to him, he would rather our vines burn to the ground than have a Russo save them. It was beyond ridiculous—I knew that much—but it was no use, trying to get him to be reasonable when it came to that family.

This morning, I walked the grounds and felt the shock course through my body at how close the fire had actually come to both of our properties. We had gotten lucky that there was no wind last night, or it would have been a completely different story, even with James battling the blaze. The only thing we had to be concerned about now was if the smoke had done any damage or not, but we wouldn't know the answer to that for months. Thankfully, the south side vines had already been harvested for the year, and they yielded the most resilient grapes; a little smoke might not have even affected them.

"It got close, huh?" The sound of James's voice made me jump and my heart skitter.

Stupid heart.

I turned toward him, using my hand to shield the sun from my eyes. "So close," I said in agreement. "Thank you again." I waved my hand in the direction of my cliff-side vines.

He smiled, and I wished I could see his eyes through his sunglasses. "You can thank me tonight."

"Tonight?" I asked, my voice cracking slightly.

"Dinner," he said.

I knew he wasn't going to give me any chance to change my mind. And to be honest, I liked that he was being so bossy, and I wondered briefly what that said about me.

"Right. Dinner. Okay," I agreed.

"I really don't want to go out of town. Do you?"

I knew what he was truly getting at. Was I okay with being seen by people who would do nothing but gossip about the two of us being together?

The idea of having to drive over an hour away in order to be surrounded by strangers seemed so ridiculous, especially when most people knew who we were anyway, simply from a business standpoint.

"I like supporting our local businesses."

He cocked a grin before saying, "Me, too. I'll pick you up at six thirty, okay?"

I couldn't speak, so I nodded, and as he walked away from me, I did nothing but watch him go.

Why did my archnemesis have to be so damn good-looking? And why was I so attracted to the one man I wasn't allowed to be with? Life wasn't fair.

As I made my way back toward my house on the property, I started thinking about my parents again. If I thought my dad was going to go crazy about James and the fire, it was going to be tenfold once he learned about the dinner date I'd agreed to go on because of it. It was pointless to pretend that James and I could keep anything to ourselves. When we'd agreed to go to dinner locally, we'd both known exactly what that meant—that the entire town would know about the date by morning. I figured that I would lie to my dad and convince him that I was just talking to James about the fire and working out logistics about potential smoke damage and how we could prepare against fire in the future. I only hoped he would buy it when the time came.

THREE KNOCKS AGAINST my wood door alerted me to the fact that James Russo was standing on the other side of it. *Should I invite him in or answer the door with my purse in hand, ready to leave?* This was new territory for me—not the dating part, but a date with the one person I wasn't even supposed to like. I had no idea how to act, and I suddenly wondered if I was overdressed as I glanced down at my heels and little black dress.

Slowly opening the door, I smiled when I saw James standing there with a bouquet of wildflowers in his hands. Everything else faded away when I looked into his blue eyes.

"Hi." He grinned, and I knew I was a goner.

How had I ever pretended to not be attracted to him?

I was sure he could see right through my facade.

"Hi." I smiled back and opened the door wider, inviting him in without thinking.

He was wearing dark slacks and a black button-up shirt that perfectly matched my outfit. We looked like we had coordinated our clothes even though we hadn't.

"These are for you."

He held out the flowers, and I took them. Our fingertips brushed, and I couldn't ignore the spark that ignited. James gave me a look, and I knew that he had just felt what I had and was searching for my confirmation, but I couldn't give it to him even if I wanted to.

There was a tremendous push-and-pull battle that warred inside me. One second, I was willing to risk it all, and the next, I was too scared to breathe wrong, afraid he'd see everything I was trying to hide.

I walked into my small kitchenette and searched in vain for a vase. I pulled out a glass pitcher and put the flowers in there, deciding that it suited them better. "They're so pretty. Unconventional."

"Just like you."

I laughed at his cheesy line because how could I not? "I'm unconventional, huh?"

"You're definitely not like any other woman," he countered.

I decided that if James thought of me that way, I definitely didn't want to change his mind.

"That'd better be some kind of compliment, Russo," I teased, playfully narrowing my eyes at him.

He took a handful of steps toward me and wrapped an arm around my waist, pulling me against him. "It's absolutely a compliment."

The way he looked at me screamed danger, and I shoved at him before moving a safe distance away. I had no idea how to navigate any of this with him. My dad's threats rang in my ears as my internal war continued to rage.

"Are you ready?" I cleared my throat as I asked.

He laughed deep and throaty, clearly enjoying how uncomfortable his presence made me. "Yeah, Julia, I'm ready." He waved an arm for me to go ahead of him. Such a gentleman.

We drove in silence toward our tiny downtown, neither of us knowing what to do. The sexual tension between us almost took on a life of its own. It felt thick and tangible, like something I could reach for and pull out of the air. My hand wanted to rest on his thigh. My fingers itched to rub the back of his neck, play with his hair, and feel the scruff of his beard. My body betrayed me with every mile, but my mind stayed firm.

When we parked, I made sure to open my door before James had a chance to. I couldn't have him reaching for my hand and interlocking his fingers with mine even though my body wanted him to and hated me for not giving in.

With James, even the simplest of gestures were dissected, overanalyzed, and stopped.

He held the front door open for me, and the hostess did a double take when she noticed it was the two of us coming in together. Her expression looked completely shell-shocked, and I couldn't blame her.

"Uh, hi, you two."

"Hi, Samantha," James and I both said in unison.

"You're here together?" she asked, her tone wary and untrusting.

James laughed as he said, "Yes. Hell has officially frozen over."

She leaned toward me and whispered in my ear, "Are you here willingly? He didn't kidnap you, did he?"

"I can hear you," James said, and Samantha genuinely looked embarrassed. "Look at her, Samantha." He waved a hand up and down the length of my body more than once. "Does this look like a woman who isn't here willingly?"

"Hey"—my voice rose, calling more unwanted attention in our direction—"what is that supposed to mean?"

"It means, you look gorgeous." James quickly covered. "And I don't think you'd dress up for a kidnapping."

My face heated with his compliment, and I knew I was blushing.

"Sorry. It's just that this is all very unexpected," Samantha apologized.

"Trust us; we know," I offered with a small smile.

"Okay, well, I'll show you to your table," she said before grabbing two menus and leading us through the restaurant where literally everyone stopped what they were doing to watch us.

A few people pulled out their phones, and I knew that they were either firing off text messages or taking pictures to send around. I suddenly wished I could hide.

What had I gotten myself into? Had I lost my mind after the fire?

"Don't you dare," James said as he pulled out my seat for me and waited for me to sit.

"Don't I dare what?" I asked as I sat slowly, as if I might change my mind at any time.

"Think about leaving."

I gave him an incredulous look. “I’m not.”

He grinned as he sat down across from me, his stupid blue eyes sparkling in the light. “You are. I don’t blame you. But don’t give in to them. Please. Just be here with me.” He sounded so sweet and sincere; I wondered how any woman ever ignored his pleas. “You promised me one date.”

“I know I did,” I said, trying to wrap my head around the fact that I’d agreed to it in the first place.

Maybe this hadn’t been the best idea. If my parents had been in town, I definitely would have said no. Them being halfway around the world had given me the confidence and freedom to say yes to James even though I knew there would still be repercussions.

“Well, well, isn’t this a pleasant surprise?” Ginny Stevens sauntered up to our table and placed a glass of water in front of each of us. She pushed her glasses up her nose and tucked her short gray curls behind her ear.

Ginny owned this restaurant with her husband, and I’d known them both for as long as I could remember. If I was right, her husband, Hank, was probably cooking tonight's meals in the back.

"Is it?" James asked her with a sweet smile.

She reached for his cheek and pinched. "Of course it is. We've all been betting on this for years." She winked before tapping the pad with her pen.

"Betting on what?" I hoped I sounded as confused as I currently felt.

She turned her attention toward me. "Betting on the two of you. We might be a small town, but we're not blind or stupid. We all knew that your parents' plan to keep you two apart would eventually backfire." She pulled out the seat between us and sat down. "To be honest, we didn't think it would take this long. We've had to start the bet over three times already. It's about time you finally showed up"—she glanced between the two of us—"together."

"I'm sorry we took so long, Ginny," James offered with a smile while I sat there with what had to be a horrified look on my face. "What was your first guess?" James asked, not at all bothered.

"I was sure you two would sneak around in high school. I had you not making it to junior year without at least one slipup. I almost won, too."

A lightbulb went off in my head. "Even you heard the rumor?"

"I knew it wasn't true. Don't ask me how, but a woman knows, and I knew."

"It wasn't true." I glared at James from across the table, wishing I had known that someone else believed me back then. I'd felt so alone at the time with no one to talk to or turn to.

"So, how long has this been going on?" James tried to change the subject, but I wanted Ginny to make him squirm a little more. He deserved it for all he'd put me through back then.

Unfortunately for me, she didn't. "For a while now."

"How long is a while?" I asked, starting to feel naive for not realizing that this had been happening behind our backs.

She laid a wrinkled hand on top of my arm. "Honey, you wouldn't have known," she started, as if reading my mind. "We obviously kept it from you both. We didn't want the bet tampered with in any way. But we started talking about it as a joke at first when you kids were in elementary school. You know, the whole *wouldn't it be funny if they ended up together* type of thing," she said with a wink before giggling. "At some point while you were in middle school, we started the first bet."

I found myself suddenly invested, wanting to know more. "Why did you have to restart it so many times?"

She swatted both of us in the arms as she rose to her feet. "Because you two kept taking too long! That's why. We had to start breaking it into intervals."

A loud laugh escaped. I couldn't help it. "Well, I hope the bet includes someone giving me a place to live for when my parents find out."

Ginny jutted out her hip. "You send your father to me if that happens. I'll remind him where he came from." She pointed her pen at me before reaching into her apron and pulling out a notepad. "Now, do you two know what you want to eat?"

We hadn't even opened the menus, but James spoke up anyway, "What are your specials tonight?"

"They're good," Ginny announced, sounding slightly annoyed that James would even have the nerve to ask.

"Then, we'll take those," he said, and she nodded, walking away.

"Any idea what we're going to be eating?" I asked with a soft laugh.

"Nope," he answered.

I lost myself in his smile before letting my eyes fall to his perfectly trimmed facial hair. That damn beard really might kill me.

"What are you looking at?" he asked, a cocky lilt in his voice.

"Your face."

"Oh. Well, keep admiring then."

I rolled my eyes as I reached for my water and took a sip, hoping to quench my desire. "I'm done."

"My turn then," he said before locking on to my eyes and licking his lips.

My body quivered before begging me to crawl across the table and right into his lap.

Stupid, stupid body, my mind scolded.

Being here with him like this was almost too much for me to rationalize. My body was determined to win this war.

"We're definitely getting caught," I said a little more nervously than I had intended.

The weight of my decision to be here with him suddenly started to bear down on me. I was out in public, with James, and was currently biting down on my bottom lip to stop myself from fantasizing about him.

"Of course we're gonna get caught. It's a small town, Julia. Everybody finds out everything."

I sucked in a quick breath, wondering which part of this he didn't seem to understand. *How could he say those words like they were no big deal; like there weren't consequences?*

"We're not supposed to be together, and I'm definitely not supposed to be anywhere with you."

How had I ever agreed to this?

My parents were going to find out, and my dad would probably fire me the second he stepped foot on California soil, if he didn't send someone to kill James first.

"Why are you so worried?" He reached his hands across the table for mine, but I moved them on top of my lap instead. He looked defeated as he leaned back and tilted his head, his blue eyes boring into mine. "Honestly, Julia, what's the worst thing that could happen? Our parents get pissed at us and what, tell us we can't be together? We're not kids anymore."

I practically choked on the air around me at his simplicity. "Well, for starters, my dad will not only fire me, but he'll kick me out of my house and disown me as well."

"He wouldn't," James said in disbelief until he saw how serious I was. "Your dad would really do all that?"

"Wouldn't yours?" I asked as my eyes started to mist over.

"I don't think so," he said incredulously.

"Well, my dad's serious when it comes to this."

"When it comes to what exactly? Keeping us apart?" He looked downright shocked, and I wondered if we were existing in the same universe at all anymore.

"Are you really this surprised?"

He reached for his glass of water and downed the entire thing before wiping his lips with his thumb. "Honestly, I am."

An annoyed huff escaped from my lips as I pinched the bridge of my nose between two fingers. "Isn't it the same over at your house? Can't imagine your dad approving of you hooking up with the La Bella girl."

"Yeah," he started as he reached for his napkin and unfolded it, "you're definitely a taboo subject, but my dad has never once threatened to take the winery away from me. I think my mom would throw a fit if he tried. That's pretty messed up, you know."

"It's kept me away from you for this long." The truth slipped from my lips before I could take it back.

I watched as his expression fell before he drew in a long breath, and his eyes lit up, as if the realization from our past years hit him all at once.

"That's why you've always stayed away from me." He moved to the seat next to mine and reached for my hand under the table. As our fingers interlocked, I squeezed them tighter instead of pulling away. "Because you were scared of losing everything, not because you weren't interested."

"I never said I was interested," I said with a grin. But I was desperate to change the subject, to steer him away from the topic of him and me because absolutely nothing for me had changed, and I didn't know how to handle it. My father would still take everything away from me without a second thought, so my feelings for James didn't matter; they couldn't. "So, did you hear about how the fire had started?"

He stared at me like he knew exactly what I was doing and why. He squeezed my hand once before releasing it and moving back to the seat across from mine. "A transformer blew, and it sparked some dry brush."

"Yeah. You caught it just in time. How did you do that, by the way?"

"I was in the barn and smelled the smoke."

"You were in the barn? Doing what?"

I'd watched James go in and out of the barn a lot when we were younger, but I never knew what exactly he did in there. He shifted in his seat and looked like he was having an internal battle, although I had no idea why.

"Tell me, James. What do you do in that barn all the time?"

He rattled the ice around in his otherwise empty water glass. "Are you sure you want to know?" He cocked an eyebrow at me.

I planted my elbows on the table and rested my chin on top of my hands in anticipation. "Tell me everything."

He hesitated before a weird look I couldn't place passed over him. "I box," he offered nonchalantly with a slight shrug.

Leaning back, I repeated, "You box? Like you have a whole setup in there or what?"

Hearing him say that for whatever reason didn't really surprise me, but now, all I could do was imagine James punching things, all shirtless and sweaty, muscles bulging.

"Oh, yeah, sure." He picked up his glass again and downed what little was left of the ice as if this topic made him uncomfortable. "I was beating the shit out of my poor punching bag when I smelled the smoke."

"How were you not exhausted after the competition?"

"I was too mad to be tired."

"Mad at what?" I knew what he had been mad about, remembered how angry he had gotten when Todd asked me out, but I was baiting him for the answer. I wanted to hear him say it out loud. I needed to hear him say that he was jealous, that he had feelings, even if I couldn't return them. It was selfish and immature, but I still pushed.

"You went out to dinner with that asshole. I couldn't stop seeing the way he looked at you." He started to sound agitated, the thought getting him all worked up again, and I hated how much I loved it. "God, I was so angry with you." His eyes crinkled around the edges, almost like he was in physical pain from just thinking about it. "I was so mad, Julia. And so fucking hurt."

My world instantly stopped spinning, the air growing heavy with his admission. This was one of those life-defining moments; I was sure of it. The kind where I was presented with two options—to either carry on per usual, lying to myself and James about my feelings for him, or cross the line that no one in our family had ever dared to cross.

I pressed my lips firmly together before admitting, "I only went out with him so that he'd stop asking."

"Kind of like what you're doing now with me?" James sounded even more offended than before, and I hated that he could even think to compare himself to someone like Todd Lestare.

"No."

"No?"

Now, he was the one pushing me on purpose. James was going to force me to say it, and I wouldn't ever be able to take it back. Once this line was crossed, we could never uncross it. I was so caught up in the moment, in the way James was looking at me, the pain in his eyes when he talked about me and Todd, that I couldn't let him continue to think the two men were one and the same in my mind.

"I actually want to be here with you," I said before clarifying, "I didn't want to be there with him."

And just like that, the world righted itself and started spinning again. The smile on James's face filled me with something I'd never felt before whenever I looked at him—hope. Could there truly be such a thing for the two of us?

"Young lady"—old man Johnson stopped at our table and gave me a pointed look—"your father would be so disappointed in you." He tsked at me before walking away.

Any hope I'd thought we might have dissolved into thin air right in front of my eyes, bitter reality replacing it in its wake.

Oh God.

What the hell had I been thinking?

I pushed away from the table, the smile on James's face instantly falling to a frown.

"Don't. Julia, don't," he begged, but it was too late.

That little comment from Mr. Johnson was all it took for me to doubt it all. I was usually so levelheaded. James had apparently made me stupid.

"I never should have come. We can't do this. Your family might not disown you for being out with me, but mine will." I reached for my purse and my coat, fumbling with them both as I tried to leave before he could stop me. "I'm sorry," I said before rushing away from him and pulling up the number for the only cab company in town.

GET THE GIRL

James

O, NO, NO, no, no, no! I paced back and forth between my seat at the table and hers.

Everyone in the restaurant was looking at me like I was half-mad. Maybe I was. I was about to throw my hands in the air and ask the gawkers for advice when Ginny appeared at my side, our dinner in her arms.

"So, I guess you want this to go?" she asked in a smart-aleck tone.

"Sure. Yes. Sorry," I said before sitting back down, my head in my hands.

I shot up in the next breath and ran, chasing Julia like my life depended on it. Hell, maybe it did. Maybe it always had.

Throwing open the front door, I burst outside, and the cool night air hit me like a slap to the face.

"Julia, please. Wait. Let me at least drive you home." I sounded broken as the words tumbled from my lips, but I didn't care. My pride was forced to take a backseat in this moment.

She turned to face me, her long, dark hair blowing in the breeze. Holding her phone toward me, she said, "I already called a cab."

Defeated, I nodded.

Why was I always losing when it came to Julia La Bella? No matter what I did or how I uncharacteristically put myself out there for her, I couldn't win.

"I really don't want you to go," I said, giving it one last shot.

I watched as she swallowed hard, her hazel eyes focusing on my feet as opposed to my face. "I know. We just can't, James. We were stupid to think we could."

The cab pulled up, and my heart sank as she moved closer to the curb.

"Just tell me one thing." My voice cracked, and she stopped moving but didn't turn around. "Why does your dad hate *me* so much? Do you even know why?"

"Because of the bet," she tossed easily over her shoulder before getting inside the car and closing the door.

I wanted to rip all my fucking hair out in my frustration. Nothing made any sense. That idiotic bet was generations old, and why our families chose to hold on to the bitterness instead of trying to get along, I'd never understand.

"But your family won it!" I shouted as the cab pulled away and disappeared out of sight, but I swore, I saw the look of surprise in her eyes.

"I DON'T KNOW, man. She looked sort of shocked when I said that her family had won the bet. It was almost like she didn't know or something." I sat on a stool in the barn, talking Dane's ear off. I'd actually called him to come over and calm me down, but he seemed to be having the opposite effect.

"Maybe she doesn't? Have you ever even thought of that?" he asked as he spun around on the chair.

I watched him spin and spin and spin, half-tempted to knock him right off. "Can you stop spinning for two seconds?"

His feet hit the ground as he came to an abrupt stop. "Killjoy."

"Child."

"So?"

He flipped me off, and I looked around for something to throw at him.

"You really think she doesn't know that her family won?"

He shrugged. "I'm just saying, what if she doesn't? Want me to go ask her?"

"No," I bit out way too quickly, and he started laughing at me. I noticed the food I'd brought back, as Ginny had insisted, sitting on the table. "Do you think I should go over and bring her dinner?"

"It would be the gentlemanly thing to do. She's probably starving over there. All alone. By herself. Stomach growling."

This time, I did grab a paintbrush and lobbed it at his head. He ducked at the last second, and I watched it bounce on the ground before skidding across the floor.

"Okay. Wish me luck."

"You need it."

"Go home," I said as I walked away, food in hand.

"Nah. You might be back soon. I think I'll wait it out. Maybe I'll paint something."

Stopping quick, I turned around. "You remember what happened the last time you touched my paints?"

He threw his hands in the air. "I was ten!"

"You painted over my mom's birthday present! You didn't even grab a clean canvas. You just painted all over the one I'd just finished. It had taken me two weeks."

"Yeah, and then you knocked me over the head with it. Took two weeks for the paint to come out of my hair."

"Good. I'd do it again," I growled.

"I won't touch your precious paints, ya big baby. Go bring the girl some food."

Instead of arguing any further with my knuckleheaded best friend, I looped the plastic bag around my fingers and headed across the darkened fields toward Julia's place. I knocked at her front door and waited. She had to know it was me, which was probably why she took her sweet time and let me stand outside in the freezing cold for so long. Maybe she thought, if she didn't answer, I'd go away.

That wasn't happening.

"Julia, come on. I know you're in there. Don't make me break your door down." I continued knocking. "I brought you food."

"Food?" she asked softly from behind the door.

I wondered how long she'd been standing there, debating on whether or not to open it for me.

"Yeah. From the restaurant. Ginny boxed it up."

The lock on the door unlatched with a loud clunking sound, and I held my breath. Her face appeared first, followed by a see-through pink robe that barely covered her tiny boy shorts and tank top. She had already changed from our date and was apparently ready for bed.

She glanced down at her bare legs before grabbing the robe and holding it tight around her middle. "I wasn't expecting you."

I wanted to grab her and pull her hard against me. I wanted to claim her lips for my own. I wanted to tell her to always fucking expect me, day or night or anytime I damn well pleased. But I didn't. Instead, I held out the bag of food and waited for her to either take it and try to slam the door in my face or invite me inside. When she opened the door wider, allowing me in, I took it as a good sign.

"Ginny would kill me if I didn't bring you yours," I said with a laugh, and she smiled. "And you know she'd ask."

"We can't have that," she said, reaching for the bag of food before disappearing into the kitchen where I noticed the flowers I'd brought her earlier were still proudly on display.

I wouldn't have been the least bit surprised if she had tossed them in the garbage the second she got home.

"About earlier," I started to say, but she put up a hand to stop me.

"No. James, it's not you. I mean"—she paused for half a breath—"it *is* you. But can I ask you something?"

It wasn't what I'd expected, her wanting to ask me a question, but I nodded. "Of course."

"What did you mean about my family winning?" She walked past me and moved toward the couch, her food plated. Once she got comfortable, I watched her take a not-so-tentative bite. "God, this is good."

"Would have been better at the restaurant with some wine," I added.

She swallowed before wiping her mouth with a paper towel. "Whose wine though?" Her head tilted as she waited for my answer.

"You know, I actually thought about that before we left. I was a little stressed out about it."

She laughed out loud. "You were? I thought about it, too, and figured I'd just do the opposite of whatever you suggested."

"Why are you so hell-bent on messing with me?" I sat down on the couch but positioned myself against the opposite corner. The last thing I wanted was to frighten her off.

"'Cause it's fun," she said before taking another bite, kicking her foot against mine like we'd done this a hundred times before instead of it being the first. "Now, about the bet."

This woman loved to maneuver the topic away from us the first chance she got.

"You really don't know?"

"Uh-uh. I mean, all I know is that your family accused us of stealing and being thieves and that apparently, you tried to ruin our name before we even had one?" she said it all like a question before offering a small shrug.

Jesus. That was the only part of the story she knew?

"First of all, *I* didn't try to do anything."

"I didn't mean you as in *you*, James Russo. I meant you as in your family." She forked another bite of food into her mouth and watched me, waiting for me to fill in all the gaps.

"I just want to be clear that whatever happened between our great-granddads all those years ago had nothing to do with you or me. If my great-grandfather did something to yours, I didn't do it. I wasn't there. You weren't there. I think this whole thing is ridiculous and has gone on for way too long. Don't you?"

She stopped chewing, as if she was carefully contemplating her words before saying them out loud to me. "I've always thought it was stupid, but then again, I don't even know what the hell we're supposed to be so mad about, aside from what I just told you. Anytime I ask my dad, he just yells and snaps at me but never gives me any more information. Sometimes, I wonder if he even knows what really went down. Why else wouldn't he just tell me?"

I shook my head. The weight of her words made me feel like I was trapped in a bad movie with no way out. How, in this century, could things still be so backward and illogical? Why were our dads so hell-bent on staying stuck in the past?

"What are you thinking?" Julia's question snapped me out of my own head.

I had no idea how long I'd been sitting there, not responding, but I noticed that her plate was clean and sitting on the coffee table in front of us. She had a glass of water in her hand and was drinking it.

"That I don't understand why our dads still hate each other. They don't have to, you know? It's all a choice, and they choose to stay mad. They choose to continue this feud for no reason other than, what? Pride? Ego?"

Julia's head nodded in what I could only assume was agreement. "I've thought about that a lot before. I think, for my dad at least, it is some twisted version of loyalty and familial obligation. His dad raised him the same way he keeps trying to raise me"—she tucked her feet up under her body—"to hate you all implicitly without questioning why."

"But you keep questioning," I said with a proud grin.

"Always have."

"That's my girl," I said without thinking, and she choked on her water, coughing and smacking at her chest. "Sorry," I said, feeling like a jerk for making her choke but not for my words. "I didn't mean," I fumbled. "I'm just proud as shit, is all."

The coughing stopped, and I felt it the moment her walls went flying back up around her. Every crack I'd made in her armor immediately fused back together, and I was shut out again. I longed to rewind the clock a mere thirty seconds, so I could stop myself from ruining the moment.

She cleared her throat, her hazel eyes glassy from choking before she took a deep breath. "First of all, I'm not your girl. Second, why are you so proud?"

I knew it—walls. "I think it's a big deal that you question your dad instead of just accepting what he tells you. That's all I meant. I like knowing that your mind isn't swayed by the thoughts of others. No matter who they are. That's a hard thing to do. And it's a respectable quality to have."

She put up a single finger. "Before you give me too much credit … I might do a lot of questioning, but I don't do a lot of standing up for it." Her hand moved to her mouth, and she played with her lips, her eyes tightening as she formulated the rest of her thoughts. I could practically see the wheels spinning. "You see, I don't agree with my dad at all on this subject, but I'm scared to death to call him out on it."

"You really think he would take the winery from you?"

How was I ever going to get inside her heart if she felt like she'd lose everything because of it?

Her long, dark hair spilled over her shoulders as she ran her fingers through it, her frustration clear. "I know it sounds ridiculous. Totally over the top, right? But you don't know my dad, James. Even if he doesn't know why he's supposed to hate you, he still does. Fiercely."

I looked around her place, my mind searching for an answer in the exposed brick of her fireplace. I wanted to fix this, fix us, or at least figure out how to give us a chance, but I had no idea how to convince her.

"You know Jeanine calls us Romeo and Juliet," she said, and I sensed her walls softening.

"Is there a version of the story where they live happily ever after instead of dying?"

A small laugh escaped from her lips. "Not that I'm aware of."

I scooted over on the couch, my body inches from hers instead of feet. "Then, I think it deserves a rewrite."

I watched as her gaze moved between my eyes and my mouth. Her tongue darted out and wet her bottom lip. The combination of the two only meant one thing; she wanted me to kiss her as much as I wanted to.

"What did you have in mind?" she asked as her eyes focused back on my lips.

I placed my hand on the back of her neck, pulling her toward me, and I let my tongue and mouth do all the talking as I prayed she wouldn't stop me. I'd been waiting for this my whole damn life.

LOVE OR LUST

Julia

H, SWEET BABY *Jesus and all of his friends. Did Jesus have friends?* It didn't matter; nothing mattered because James's lips felt like home.

The man was skilled, kissing me softly yet firmly. He was slow in his movements but aggressive as well, and I had no idea how one man could command so many contradictory feelings with his mouth, but he did.

I knew immediately that my body would bend and curve to his whim, his hands controlling our pace, his tongue fueling our mutual desire. I couldn't remember the last time someone had made me feel this alive, like a lit fuse on the end of a firework ready to explode. To be honest, I didn't think I'd ever felt quite like this before. Hell, with James's tongue in my mouth, I could barely remember the last time I'd had sex. That wasn't true. I definitely remembered it, but it was so awful that I wished I could forget.

I should have hated how comfortable being in this position with him was, but I found myself craving more. Kissing James was supposed to repulse me, remind me that I was in enemy territory, but it only made me want to kiss him more. And, when he lifted me up like I weighed nothing, tossing my robe to the floor before carrying me back into my bedroom, I should have fought against what was coming instead of practically fiending for it.

Truth be told, I considered stopping what was about to happen for all of twenty seconds. Then, his fingers brushed along my inner thigh, and I forgot that I was supposed to hate him. All I wanted was more; my body reacted, my pulse quickened, and my heart raced. Add in the fact that I'd been fighting my attraction and desire for this man for the majority of my life, and you had a ticking time bomb ready to explode between my thighs.

I didn't want to fight it anymore.

But I really didn't want to hate myself for giving in either.

"I've thought about this at least a thousand times," he said as he pressed kisses against my neck before his teeth nibbled on my ear.

"You have?" I asked breathlessly.

He stopped moving and looked at me, those blue eyes shining. "Haven't you?"

"I might have had some fantasies starring your beard," I admitted.

He bit his bottom lip before running a hand across it. "My beard, huh?"

I placed my hand on top of his and moved across his jawline. "Yeah. It's sexy as hell."

"Good to know." He grinned. "This has starred in my fantasies," he said before his thumb ran down the length of my neck. "You have the sexiest neck." He leaned in and pressed kisses there before moving lower. "And your shoulders. God, I've wanted to bite them for years," he said.

I giggled. "My shoulders?"

"Stop repeating my words, Julia," he said.

I found myself shutting right up. Normally, I'd get a lot of joy out of arguing with him, but I liked this bossy version too much to do anything that might make him stop. His fingers moved along the curves of my body under my tank, my skin prickling to life with each touch.

He reached for the hem of my top and tugged it up toward my head. I ducked out from it and heard his breath hitch. I was completely exposed from the waist up, and it was exhilarating to see the look in his eyes as he stared at me. I'd never had any self-esteem issues when it came to my body, but seeing the way James looked at me was something else entirely. He made me feel beautiful and wanted without saying a single word.

"I've wanted to touch your skin and taste you for as long as I can remember, Julia. I don't know how I've lived this long without doing either." His lips pressed against my chest before lowering to my breasts. He kneaded one nipple between his fingertips while his mouth did work on the other. His tongue rolled across my breast as his teeth bit down, eliciting a pain that didn't hurt, but made me cry out all the same.

"God, James." My voice came out sounding so heady. I should have been embarrassed, but I was too turned on.

"Did I hurt you?" he asked but didn't stop.

My fingers wrapped in his dark hair and pulled. "No."

His lips lowered to my stomach where I felt my abs constrict and release with each breath.

"Your hips are so sexy. You have perfect curves." He bit down on my hip bone before swirling his tongue around the bite mark.

I had no idea what he was doing, but I loved every second. It felt like no inch of my skin would remain untouched by the time James was done with me.

I let go of his hair with my right hand and moved it on top of his shoulder. The way his muscles flexed and strained was so sexy; I found myself squeezing his arm, my nails digging into his skin.

"I like the way you feel. Your muscles are so hard." It was an idiotic thing to say, but I'd never touched James before, and I liked how solid he felt.

His head shot up to glance at me before he refocused back on my body, worshipping it. He brushed his tongue against my hip before moving lower, taking my shorts and panties with him. Before I could say a word or move or even think, James was between my thighs, the way I'd imagined so many times before. The feel of his beard against my legs was heaven, but it was nothing like the way it felt to have his tongue inside me.

"Jesus, Julia, you taste so fucking good."

My mouth dropped open with his words. Of course I wanted him to think that, but hearing him say it catapulted me to another level. My thighs spread open wider as he got more comfortable there, his fingers swiping up and down before he inserted them inside me.

"You feel amazing," I said out loud.

He moaned against me, his hot breath heating my core. His tongue darted in and out before he sucked my clit, making me squirm. A strong arm shot across my stomach, firmly holding me in place. Apparently, I moved too much, and he wanted me to stop. Sucking in a few quick breaths, I tried to steady myself, but it was no use. That man's tongue was doing work in ways that didn't make sense; there was no way my body could relax. I bucked against him, my hips rising into his mouth as I started my climax.

"I want to taste you when you come," he said.

That was all it took for me to give myself over and completely release. I shuddered and jerked as his tongue went wild, licking and sucking until I couldn't take anymore, and I pushed his head away from me with a laugh.

"Stop. Please stop."

James moved to a sitting position and wiped his mouth with the back of his hand, his beard glistening in the light. His eyes shimmered with mischief as he reached behind me and pulled me up to face him. "God, you're beautiful," he said before his hand wrapped around my neck, and he kissed me, the taste of me all over his tongue.

I hesitated for only a second before I was all in, my tongue in his mouth, my lips merging with his. I couldn't get enough of him.

When he let me go, I fell back onto the bed and watched as he removed his clothes, pulling a condom out from somewhere and rolling it onto his length. I almost offered to do it, but I wasn't that bold yet. As he moved on top of me, the tip of his dick positioned at my entrance, I lifted my hips to try to force him inside. He laughed, knowing full well that he was in control, and I lowered my hips back down to the bed and waited.

"Are you going to make me beg?" I asked, pretending to be annoyed.

"No. I just wanted to look at you first," he said.

My heart melted into my mattress, never to beat the same again. We stayed that way, staring into each other's eyes for what felt like a full minute or two, but I was certain it wasn't. And, when he moved inside me, neither one of us broke eye contact.

It was so intimate, so utterly connecting. I felt like more than just my skin was bared to him; my soul was in the open, free for the taking. The most reassuring part was that I knew innately that he felt the same way.

My body stretched for him as he entered me, slowly filling me. Even in my most perfect dreams, it hadn't felt this way. I couldn't have known. I didn't know anything could even feel like this, this all-encompassing, this emotional. He pumped in and out of me, slowly at first before his pace started to quicken, and my hands were all over his shoulders, his arms, and his chest again. I couldn't stop squeezing, pulling, wanting him closer.

I lost myself in the way his body moved with mine, how receptive he was and how much he paid attention. If I flinched for even a second, he was aware of it and adjusted. And, when I tossed a leg around his lower back, he moved it off and told me no. James was a thousand times better at sex than I was. He made me feel like I'd never done it before. At least, not properly.

Maybe this is something more than just sex, I started to wonder but stopped myself from going that far, that fast.

"Are you okay?" He rolled his hips against mine, and I nodded before he leaned down to kiss me. "You feel amazing. So tight. So hot," he said between kisses. "I've wanted this my whole life."

He continued to kiss me with so much passion that I thought we might explode. I felt the weight of his words, the depth of his emotions with every touch of his tongue.

"I didn't know it could feel this way." I circled my hips against his, creating friction and feeling my orgasm rise.

"It's because it's us, Julia. It wouldn't be like this with anyone else. It couldn't be." He kissed me more as his pace quickened. I felt him grow bigger inside me, and I knew what was about to happen. "Oh, babe, I'm gonna come."

"I know. I feel it," I breathed against his neck, and he nudged me.

"Look at me," he demanded. "Don't look away. Don't close your eyes."

I didn't respond with words, but I did what he'd asked. And, when he came inside me, I felt everything he was feeling by looking in his eyes. His body shuddered on top of me, his sexy groans filling every empty nook of my house. I watched as his chest heaved and his muscles moved between flexing and relaxing. The man was a god, but I'd be damned if I admitted that to him. Doing this had been crossing the line enough.

He rolled off of me and onto his back but grabbed me in the movement. Without warning, I was in his arms, my head lying on his chest as he played with my damp hair.

"Don't ruin the moment and talk shit about the fact that I want to cuddle with you after," he instructed, his breathing erratic and uneven.

I laughed against his chest and got lost in the sound of his heart beating. "I wasn't going to say a thing." But I had been thinking it.

THE SOUND OF shouting and arguing invaded my dream, waking me from it. I blinked a few times before piecing together that it was the familiar sound of both my and James's dads yelling at each other. I'd lost count the number of times they had screamed and threatened one another over the years. I tried to move before realizing that I was tangled with James's naked body, our legs and arms intertwined. God, he was warm. I'd forgotten for a millisecond that last night even happened, but the sound of my dad's voice yelling reminded me.

Wait.

Why was my Dad back in the states?

A loud, hard knock on the door, followed by my dad shouting my name, had me violently shaking James awake.

"James! James, you have to hide." My eyes practically bugged out of my head as I shot out of bed.

"Hide?" he repeated like he wasn't sure if I was serious or not as he fought back a yawn.

"My dad is here. He can't see you. I don't know what he'd do. I'm not playing." My expression was stone-cold serious, my eyes pleading with him as I pulled my long hair into a ponytail before twisting it into a bun. I reached for my pajamas and quickly got dressed.

"Tell me where to go," he said, finally understanding the gravity of the situation.

I looked around before pointing toward the closet, and James hopped out of bed and tucked himself in there. I hated that I felt like a teenager who was doing something wrong, but now wasn't the time for logic.

"Julia!" my dad shouted again.

I yelled back at him to wait a minute. My stomach twisted as I opened the front door, and my dad barged inside.

"What took you so long?"

"I was sleeping. What are you doing home?"

"Where is he?"

Oh my gosh. Does he know James is here? There is no way he could know, I thought, convincing myself as I stood a little taller.

"Where is who?"

"I know you went out with that boy last night."

"It was just dinner, Dad."

"How many times have I told you to stay away from him? I've warned you. Stay away from that boy, Julia. You will not see him again," he shouted, his voice filled with so much rage.

I hated how misplaced his anger was. James hadn't done anything to our family, so why did he have to pay?

"I won't? This is ridiculous, Dad. We're both adults," I attempted to stand up for myself, but my dad leveled me with a look that reminded me how serious this was.

He poked his head in the kitchen before looking in my bathroom and heading into my bedroom. I followed him, hot on his heels, half-terrified that he was about to find James naked inside my closet.

"What are you doing? My room's a disaster."

Thankfully, he walked back into the living room before facing me. "You've always had a crush on him."

"No, I haven't," I tried to argue, but it felt useless at this point. Apparently, I hadn't been as good at hiding my emotions as I'd thought.

"Anyone with eyes can see the way you look at him. The way you've always looked at him," he said accusingly.

I flushed, knowing that James could hear every word.

"He's not what you think," I started to explain, wanting my dad to give him a chance, to maybe see things differently for once.

"Is he a Russo?" my dad cut me off, and I nodded. "Then, that's all I need to know. Why can't you just listen? Russos cannot be trusted, Julia. Do you think this boy actually likes you?"

My mouth fell slightly agape as I struggled to find the words to combat his accusations without confessing my sins from last night.

"Oh, you do. That's rich. You think he actually cares about you?"

My dad laughed, and I couldn't remember ever feeling so small or stupid before. It would be one thing to hear this crap from a jealous girl or a guy like Todd Lestare, but to hear it from my own father was a little more than unnerving and hurtful.

"He's a good man."

I half-wished James would appear at my side and stand up to my dad with me, but I knew that would only cause further chaos. This was something I needed to do on my own. Plus, the poor guy was probably rocking in the corner of my closet, wondering how he'd gotten into this mess in the first place. James was going to bolt and never look back after this and I wouldn't blame him.

"Anything that boy does is for his own benefit."

"Why would you say that? You don't even know him." I plopped down on the couch, my feelings all over the place. My head spun with words like *betrayal* and *disloyalty* while my heart beat with the exact opposite, happy I had finally given in to it.

"And, after one dinner, you think you do? Russos lie and manipulate to get what they want. It hasn't worked in their favor yet, and I'll be damned if it works on my watch!"

"What can James possibly want from me?" I asked through my wonder.

"Our vines," my dad growled in response.

I refused to accept his opinions so easily. Not this time. "He has his own."

"You know the south side vines are different. No one has those. They've been trying to steal them for years. I can't imagine they'd stop now."

"Dad."

"See him again, and you're out." His face hardened. "Don't test me, Julia."

He walked out of my tiny cottage and slammed the door behind him, making the pictures on my walls rattle. I sank into the cushions of my couch and put my head in my hands.

"Well, that was fun." James's voice scared the crap out of me, and I jumped, my nerves completely frayed. He peered out one of the tiny windows before turning the lock on the door. "You weren't joking." He sat down next to me on the couch before wrapping an arm around my shoulders and pulling me against him. "The hate runs deep."

"How much did you hear?"

"Pretty sure I heard every word." He pressed a kiss to the side of my head. "I only enjoyed the parts where he talked about you having a crush on me. The rest was awful."

I forced a smile before turning my body to face him. "I don't have a crush on you," I pretended to argue, but there was no use, especially after last night.

"Well, I sure as hell have one on you," he said without an ounce of shame, and I wished I had his bravery. "So, how are we going to fix this?" he asked.

I gave him a confused look. "What do you mean?" There was nothing to fix.

"Julia"—he grabbed my hand and held it—"I want to be with you. Last night was incredible. Can you really walk away from what we've started?"

"You heard what my dad said." My eyes began to water, and the last thing I wanted to do was cry in front of James.

"We'll change his mind." He sounded so confident, like what he suggested was the easiest solution in the world. "We'll make him see how happy we are and that I'm not trying to con you out of anything."

"We can't," I said, knowing that my dad would not listen to anything a Russo had to say.

"We can."

"He won't listen."

My father was not a compassionate or understanding man.

"We haven't even tried yet," he said, his tone reasonable and logical—another two qualities my father lacked.

"It's just—" I choked on my words, my thoughts, and my emotions as he stood up from the couch, looking like a knight in shining armor. “This is all happening too fast,” I lied.

“Too fast?” James’s eyes practically rolled out of his head. “I’ve been in love with you since I was a kid. There’s nothing slower than the story of us.”

“I’m sorry.” I stood up and started pacing. “You have to go.” Then, I began freaking out. “But make sure no one sees you. Can you do that?”

His head lowered, and my shining knight’s armor looked tarnished and defeated. “I don’t want to lose you.”

“It was one night, James. You never had me.” My words were harsh and bitter. I hated myself for telling the lie, but it was the only way to get him to leave, and I needed him to do that.

But, as my plan worked, I watched him go, wondering what the hell I’d just done as my heart berated me with every beat inside my chest.

HEARTBREAKER

James

IF I'D THOUGHT that Julia La Bella couldn't break my heart again, I was dead wrong. I thought I'd heard the damn thing crack in half with her words. I sure as hell felt it as I made my way out her door and snuck into the far part of the vineyard where I hopefully wouldn't be seen by anyone. But, to be honest, part of me wanted to get caught.

I ran into my mom the second I opened our front door.

"Oh, James, are you just getting in?" She looked me up and down.

"I was just in the barn," I said as I made my way past her.

My parents had added onto the house and now lived in a giant, detached master suite downstairs, which left the entire second floor at my disposal. They gave me my privacy, and I gave them theirs.

"Sure, honey," she said, clearly seeing through my lie.

Thankfully, she didn't question me further.

I walked up three stairs before stopping short. "Hey, Mom?"

"Yes?"

"Do the La Bellas even know about the bet?" I didn't need to elaborate or fill in the blanks. My mom knew exactly what I was asking.

"I have always assumed so." She looked at me with slight confusion in her eyes.

"You've never talked to Mrs. La Bella before, have you?"

My mom glanced around the room to make sure my dad couldn't hear. "Not really, but I've always wanted to. We aren't allowed to be friends either, you know." It was easy to forget that Julia and I weren't the only ones suffering the consequences of our dads' feud. "Why do you ask about the bet?"

"It was just something Julia mentioned the other day in passing. I don't think she knows any of it, except the parts where Great-grandfather tried to take it back from her family."

She offered me a nonchalant shrug. "That seems a little far-fetched, but I guess I wouldn't know."

The bet had happened on both of our paternal sides. Julia was the first girl born in our two families since the rivalry had begun. A romantic relationship between the Russos and La Bellas hadn't ever been an option before now, which was why I was sure her dad had raised her with threats to stay away from me.

"I thought so, too, but I don't think she was lying."

"You know, I guess it would make sense," my mom started to say, her mind clearly spinning in a new direction.

"How so?"

"If you only pass down the parts where you were done wrong, then it keeps the feud alive. The hatred and anger seem justified. I can see how, over the years, certain parts got dropped from their side of the story."

"Yeah, I guess I could see that," I agreed before getting slightly agitated. "But it kind of makes it all worse."

"What do you mean?"

"The fact that they don't even know the whole story and choose to live their lives with this total contempt for our existence." I started to get fired up, my emotions getting the best of me as I thought back to all the words Mr. La Bella had said about me.

"You know, James, just for the record"—my mom offered me a sly smile before backing away—"I've always liked Julia. She's a smart girl. Talented. Motivated."

She disappeared into the kitchen before even waiting for my response. Hearing my mom approve of Julia was a gift I'd never known I needed or wanted.

I headed up the rest of the stairs, pausing when I noticed Dane asleep in the guest room, the bedroom door wide open. He'd stayed the damn night, and I hadn't even noticed his car, not that I had been looking for it. I was too busy trying not to get shot, weaving through the La Bella property. After hearing Julia's dad this morning, I'd figured he'd be all too willing to shoot me first and ask questions over my dead body later.

I decided to wake Dane up. Walking over to his bed, I shook his shoulders and said his name three times. He started to stir before his eyes shot open.

"Dude. Finally." He reached for his phone and looked at it. "You stayed the night? Are you just getting back?" Sitting straight up, he wiped his eyes. "What happened? Tell me. Did you hook up?"

Even though I'd willingly set myself up for this, he asked way too many questions.

"Her dad came home." I decided I'd start with that little fact nugget.

"Shit. Did he see you? Are you dead right now?" He pushed my chest with his finger. "Okay. Not ghost James. Go on."

"We talked, and I'm pretty sure she knows about twenty percent of our families' history. I'd always assumed that she knew the whole thing. I'd never understood why she hated my family so much when it should have been the other way around, but I'd accepted it. Like a fool, I'd just accepted it all without fighting or questioning it."

"I knew it. I knew she didn't know." He snapped his fingers like he had just stumbled on some world-altering knowledge. "So, did you tell her the whole story?"

"I started to, but then she started talking about *Romeo and Juliet*, and I might have gotten a little distracted."

I refused to fill Dane in on every single detail of the night I'd shared with Julia. Some things were private, and even though I'd told him everything in the past, this time felt different. I cared about her too much to lay it all out there.

Dane let out a loud laugh as he adjusted the pillow behind his back. "Shit. How have I never put that together before? You guys are the damn Montagues and Capulets in present-day form. Why did they hate each other anyway? Same reason as you guys? A bad bet gone wrong?"

And, now, Dane was completely distracted.

"I have no idea. Read the book and get back to me," I said, trying my best to sound annoyed. "Can you please focus?"

"Stop yelling at me. Someone didn't get any last night." He yawned. "Tell me you at least kissed the girl," he said, his tone filled with hope more than anything else.

I nodded in response. When his face practically lit up, I had to stop myself from grinning back.

"And then what? Her dad came over and cockblocked the rest?"

"He didn't show up until this morning. I might have had to hide in the closet," I said, completely fucking embarrassed as I burned a hole in the carpet instead of looking at his face.

"Might have?" he asked, holding back his laughter.

"Fine"—I looked right at him—"I definitely had to hide in the closet."

He exploded, the laughter spilling out. "I'm sorry, but I can't." He continued to laugh, his entire body shaking. "Oh, man. So, now, what? Will you see her again, or was it a one-time, get-it-out-of-your-system kind of thing?"

My insides instantly raged. A one-time thing with Julia had never been my intention. "You know it's not like that."

"I know it's not for you, but was it for her? Did you even ask? Are you guys on the same page?"

I suddenly grew nervous as Julia's last words played out in my head. *"It was one night, James. You never had me."*

Hearing them repeat, if only in my mind, was just as brutal as hearing them spill from her lips the first time. My chest instantly ached.

"We didn't get a chance really. Her dad threatened her. He reminded her to stay away from me. Then, she kicked me out, and here I am."

Dane's brows pulled together. "Her dad threatened her? How?"

This was one thing I had no qualms about sharing, so I filled him in on everything I'd overheard from the closet. Dane's expression turned as shocked as I was sure mine had been before it changed again into something unreadable.

"And you're sure you didn't hear him wrong, misinterpret this somehow?"

"I'm sure."

His eyes darted around the room as his head shook in what had to be disbelief. "Wow. I think he might hate you more than your dad hates her."

"I don't think there's any comparison, to be honest. My dad's never said anything even remotely close to the things her dad said to her."

"Who would disown their own kid? That's severely messed up."

Dane started to shift uncomfortably, and I felt his pain. I knew it well. I'd been living it for as long as I could remember.

"I know, but"—I paused and wrung my hands together—"what do I do about it?"

He instantly straightened. "What do you want to do about it?"

"I want the girl," I said without thinking, but it was the truth, so I didn't take it back.

"Then, let's get her," he said with a big-ass smile, and I found myself almost believing that it was truly possible.

"How?" I asked because we needed a plan.

"Good question." He started tapping a finger against his chin while he thought. "You can show up with a ring and propose."

"Uh ..." I craned my neck and looked at him like he was insane. Because, clearly, he was.

"I'm just saying that you could skip all the stuff in between and get right to the good part," he offered with a shrug.

"Yeah, that's not even remotely a good plan, let alone a sane one."

"I'm just trying to help," he said all innocent-like, and I groaned, hoping for a new idea. "Okay. Make her jealous then."

My interest suddenly kicked up a few dozen notches, my ego obviously a fan of this kind of idea. "Go on."

"Ask Jeanine out," he suggested, and I shot him a look that said I'd rather die than cross that line. "Fine. Ask out every other woman in town and make sure she hears about it. It will drive her so crazy that she'll come running over here with open arms and hop in your lap."

My heart plummeted inside my chest as reality smacked me like a two-by-four. “No, she wouldn’t. She didn’t come running when I dated in the past. Trying to make her jealous would just give her a reason to stay away. Maybe, if we were still in high school, I’d go that route, but not now. What else you got?”

He laughed before clasping his hands together. “Uh, you could finally make a better wine than her and win a competition for once.”

“Dick,” I muttered under my breath because we both knew that Julia had something that I didn’t when it came to creating the perfect blends.

Dane cupped his ear and leaned forward. “What? Didn’t quite catch that.”

“Even if I did somehow beat her in the next competition, how would that win her over?”

“I don’t know. Maybe she’d be so pissed that she lost to you that she’d want to know what you did to win. Knowing Julia, she wouldn’t leave your side until you told her everything. You’d have her following you around the winery until you confessed it all.”

Dane was absolutely right, and I found myself smiling at the thought of a fired-up Julia hot on my heels, demanding to know exactly how I'd beaten her. It wasn't the worst idea in the world even if it was damn near impossible.

"We'll add that to the list."

"Shit, am I supposed to be writing this down?" he asked as he reached for his phone and started typing frantically on the screen.

"Yes. Now, what else?" I waited for more asinine ideas from Dane that would hopefully trigger the right one in me. Sometimes, brainstorming with other people was the best way to figure out what direction you needed to take.

NO LONGER A LA BELLA

Julia

AFTER JAMES LEFT this morning, I cried in my bathroom. It was as if every emotion that I'd held back my entire life came pouring out in those moments while I held my knees against my chest and rocked back and forth. I never expected to feel so much in the aftermath, but giving myself over to him, the one person who I was forbidden from even speaking to, was a whole new level of ... well, *everything.*

I knew that I had been attracted to James before, but I'd had no idea that having sex with him would make me feel the way that I currently did, like my world had shifted. My reality seemed rearranged, different somehow. And it wasn't because of the fact that us being together was supposed to be wrong. To be honest, no other guy had ever felt more right. James and I were connected now, in ways neither one of us could take back or erase, not that I would.

Apparently, it wasn't only our bodies that had intertwined last night. Something deeper had also shifted, and a new bond had formed. I could feel it living and breathing inside of me, begging for more of James, itching for permanence.

But I couldn't give it what it needed.

After pulling myself together and one last swipe under my eyes to dry the tears, I decided to distract myself with work even though it was technically my day off. Winning the competition meant that I had a new limited-edition stamp to make and a new wine to bottle, and I was excited to get started.

I still hadn't unpacked my car from the other day, and I needed to do that first before I could head into the bottling barn. The second I rounded the corner for my car, I saw James and his father on opposite sides of the barn. Chills raced down the length of my body as I tried to pretend like I was unaffected by his presence and didn't notice him.

James cleared his throat, but I refused to make eye contact. He did it again, but I still resisted. My dad would come unglued if he saw us talking, especially after the warning he'd doled out this morning. Plus, seeing his dad out there made me nervous as well.

How would he react to the idea of us being friendly? I wondered.

"Are you really going to pretend like you don't see me?" he shouted across our lots, and that got my attention.

I cast him a wicked glare before glancing to see if his dad was watching us or not. He wasn't, but if looks could kill, I knew mine would have knocked James right on his ass.

Was he insane? Was he trying to get me in trouble?

I pressed the button on my remote and watched the trunk pop open, ignoring James even though I could see that he had stopped whatever he was doing and was facing my direction.

"We're back to this? Are we really back to this?"

Glancing at him once more, I softened, my eyes pleading for him to please be quiet when the sound of my parents' front door opened. I didn't even have to look up to know my dad was coming. I'd long ago memorized the sound of his feet slamming against the ground with every step.

"Julia, get inside the house."

"Dad, stop. It's not what you think." I swallowed around the ball now firmly lodged in my throat because it was exactly what my dad thought.

"Get inside the house now!"

His stubby finger pointed toward the door, and I reluctantly followed his demand, once again feeling like a child. I opted for one last look in James's direction, and it was my downfall. He was watching my every move, and my dad was watching us both, the anger on his face growing by the second.

The moment I walked inside the open front door, I heard the shouting. It was Mr. Russo and my dad screaming at each other, but I wasn't sure about what exactly. Their voices rose, and when I moved to look out the window, I saw the two men in each other's faces and at each other's throats. I wondered if this would be the day that they physically came to blows. James jumped between them, holding them at arm's length apart. The shouting continued, and just when I thought I couldn't take it anymore and was about to head out there, the two men kicked dirt at one another before my dad stalked away, heading straight for me.

I didn't know what to do with myself as my nerves ran ragged. When my dad entered the house, his face was an unnatural shade of red, and I couldn't remember the last time I'd seen him this mad.

"Pack your things, Julia."

My stomach felt like it dropped to my knees as bile instantly rose in my throat. "What? Dad, you can't be serious." I looked around the room, scanning the house for any sign of my mother.

Where the hell is she? I wondered to myself.

She wouldn't let this happen without some kind of fight, would she?

I honestly had no idea what my mom would do in this situation. I knew she would feel in the middle, but whose side would she take?

"I warned you," my dad bit out, his voice cold as ice and devoid of any emotion. "I told you to stay away from him, and you purposely defied me. You think I can't tell what's going on? The one thing, Julia," he said as he pinned me with the harshest look, "the one thing I've asked of you. You will not humiliate this family any further. You obviously don't understand the concept of loyalty even though I raised you on it. I'm sure your great-grandfather is turning over in his grave right now. Get your things and get out."

My eyes started to water, and I knew my dad would consider it weak if I cried in front of him over this, but I couldn't stop the tears from spilling over if my life depended on it. "Where am I supposed to go?"

"That isn't really my problem, now is it?"

He reached for a sandwich sitting on the counter that I hadn't noticed before. I watched as he moved it toward his mouth and took a bite, as if he didn't have a care in the world. He chewed the bread and meat like he hadn't just kicked his sole daughter out of the only house she'd ever known. He sat there, chewing and swallowing his food, and

I couldn't imagine ever eating again. My stomach rolled with the thought.

"Not sure what you're still standing here for."

I stumbled out of the back door and toward the guesthouse. Once inside, I grabbed a large duffel bag from the same closet James had hidden in this morning. *God, had it really only been a handful of hours ago*? It seemed like days. All the feelings and emotions James had incited within me felt so far removed now.

Glancing around, I wasn't sure where to start. How many clothes would I need? How long was I going to be gone, and was I ever going to be allowed to come back here? I had no idea, and I should have reached for a suitcase instead, but I was too overwhelmed and shocked to think clearly.

Throwing random clothes and toiletries into the bag as fast as I could, I dialed Jeanine's number and pressed the phone against my shoulder with my head.

"What's up, hot stuff?" she answered, her voice cheery.

The tears continued to spill as I struggled to find my voice. "Hey. Can I stay with you for a bit?" My breathing was erratic.

"Are you crying? Julia? What happened?" Her questions were frantic, but before I could respond, she continued, "But, of course, you can stay here. Do you need me to come get you?"

"No. I'll be there soon." My breath hitched and skipped audibly as I tried to sound as though my chest wasn't shaking.

"Did James do something to you? I'll hurt him. String him up by his balls in front of town hall."

I wanted to laugh, but it died somewhere deep inside me. "I'll tell you everything when I"—I paused to hiccup—"get there, okay?"

"Okay." Her voice sounded so worried. "Drive safe. Park in my guest spot. Stay as long as you need."

"Thank you," I managed to get out before ending the call. I knew she'd forgive me for the abruptness of it all.

Glancing around my place, I decided that I could always buy or borrow anything that I forgot to pack. I was scared that if I took too long to leave, my dad would force me to go with only the clothes on my back. I still couldn't believe that he was doing this. This had always been my biggest fear, and now, it was coming true. I'd always believed my dad's threats were real, but a part of me was still shocked that he'd actually followed through with them. Had I really done something so awful that it warranted this type of punishment?

I got into my car and started the engine before waiting a few seconds to see if anyone would come and stop me. Maybe my mom would appear from wherever she was, tell me this was all some huge misunderstanding and that she'd try to fix it. But, when no one came, I accepted the truth and stepped on the gas pedal.

Driving to Jeanine's apartment downtown was a feat in itself. My eyes had never been so blurry before, the road appearing and disappearing with each blink. Thankfully, I got there in one piece and didn't hurt anyone else in the process, partly because I'd pulled over twice and waited until I could get back onto the road safely.

Navigating into the familiar guest spot, I turned off the engine, reached for my duffel, and trudged up the stairs to the second floor. The door opened before I could even raise my hand to knock, and Jeanine pulled me into a bear hug, which of course caused the tears to start falling all over again.

"Get in here. Tell me everything."

So, I did.

I told her about our dinner date. When I asked her about the bet that everyone in town seemed to be in on, she claimed she had never heard of it before, and I believed her. I begrudgingly continued and told her about my bolting in the middle of dinner, to which she called me a chickenshit, but then she changed her tune after learning that it'd led to James showing up at my front door with food in hand and one unforgettable night in bed. She called me a genius then.

I moved onto her oversize couch as she continued to stand, clearly too wound up by everything I'd just told her to sit still. Her sofa was the kind of worn-in piece that hugged your body the second you sat down in it. Reaching for a blanket, I tucked my legs underneath my butt and covered myself up as she stood with her hands on her hips, listening to me talk. Her eyes filled with moisture when I told her what had happened with my dad. She'd been a fixture at our house, growing up, so it really hurt her to hear this part of the story, especially when she hadn't known anything about the threats up until the other day when I confessed them to her. I'd done a spectacular job of keeping some familial things to myself.

"I didn't believe you when you told me before. I mean, I believed you, but I figured that you were exaggerating. Does that make me a bad friend?" She pulled out one of her barstools and sat down.

"No, but I'm not really the exaggerating type," I said, a little defensive.

"I know you're not. It's just that the idea of your dad kicking you out is hard for me to wrap my head around. It's too insane. Too irrational. Not that your dad isn't crazy, but actually making you leave your home is."

"I know."

"Where was your mom during all this?"

"I have no idea. I don't even know if she was home or not."

"She's not going to just let your dad do this, Julia. Do you think?"

I honestly had no idea what my mom would do once she found out. "I never thought my dad would *really* kick me out in the first place, so I'm not sure. I mean, does she stand by her man, or does she tell him he's being unreasonable?" I offered a noncommittal shrug. "I guess it could go either way."

"This really is *Romeo and Juliet* come to life," she said.

I couldn't even disagree this time or joke back that it was nothing like that.

"I guess you're not allowed to go to work?" Jeanine knew that the winery was my life. It was both of our livelihoods. "Wait, does this mean I'm out of a job, too?" Her face pinched with pain, and I realized that I didn't have an answer for her. "Not that it matters. I just need to know if I'm supposed to show up tomorrow or not."

"I honestly have no idea. But, yeah, you should definitely show up. If my dad wants you gone, make him say it to your face," I said, my spirit feeling a little less weak and a little more fired up.

"Well, you know that you can stay here as long as you need. I already made up the guest room for you. And sharing a bathroom will be fun. Right?"

She pulled her hair back and tied it into a little knot that looked cute. I'd tried that once before and ended up looking like a balding rat.

"Yeah. It will be like we're sisters. We can fight over makeup and counter space and stuff." I offered up a smile for the first time.

Jeanine moved from the barstool over to the couch, and I watched it swallow her as she sat down.

"Do you think James knows what happened? Like, do you think he saw you leave?"

"I have no idea."

"Well, are you going to tell him?"

"I wasn't planning on talking to him ever again," I said, and I meant it.

He was the whole reason I was in this mess in the first place. Because of him, I'd broken the only hard rule I'd ever been given in my life. And in doing so, I'd lost everything.

"Oh, so you're just going to pretend like last night never happened?" she asked skeptically.

"I've done it before. It's not that hard," I reminded her, referring to the one-night stand I'd had six months back. After it was over, I'd wiped it from my mind and never thought about it again.

"It wasn't with James before."

"James doesn't change anything," I said, trying to convince myself that it was the truth.

"James changes everything." She rolled her eyes at me and huffed out a long breath. "Can you at least be honest with yourself?"

Her tone was soft, and it sent me right over the emotional cliff that I'd been barely hanging on to.

"No." I sat there, shaking my head back and forth. "I can't be honest with myself. Because being with James isn't an option for me. So, I have to lie to you, to me, to anyone who asks. I have to pretend like I don't want him. I have to convince myself that he doesn't matter."

Her face scrunched together. “You already lost your job, Julia. You don’t have to lose the guy, too.”

Her statement rang with a certain air of truth that I didn’t want to accept. I couldn’t allow myself to believe that the winery was lost to me forever. It couldn’t be gone for good. I wanted to be able to go back home and run what I was entitled to.

“I’m not willing to give up the winery just yet.”

“I understand that. I just think you should be able to have both. There has to be a way. Don’t you think there’s got to be some sort of compromise?”

I looked around before pointing at my duffel bag on the ground, reminding her exactly why I was here in the first place. “It doesn’t look like it.”

“So, you’d really be okay with sacrificing your dream guy for your job?”

A guttural laugh escaped from my throat. “My dream guy? And it’s not just any job, Jeanine. It’s my family. It’s our legacy. It’s what I’ve worked for my whole life. I was raised on our winery and always knew it would be mine one day. If it doesn’t stay in the family, then where does it go?”

She didn't hide her disapproval. "Maybe your dad should have thought about that before kicking you out and making this ridiculous demand."

I could tell she was holding something else back. I could see it written all over her face, so I prompted her. "Just say it."

She raised her eyebrows and gave me a look.

"I know there's more spinning in that head of yours. Spit it out already."

Her lips pursed as she admitted, "Just hear me out first before you interrupt, okay?" she asked, and I nodded. "I think you could have both. I think you could have James and still work at a winery. You're insanely talented, and any number of companies would be thrilled to have you on their team. Hell, they'd probably start World War Three, trying to compete over you. You have to stop acting like your family's is the only gig in town. If you love making wine and doing what you do so much, you can realistically do it somewhere else. You're just being stubborn and scared."

I started to speak up, and she held five fingers in the air to stop me.

"Eh. You promised." I closed my mouth, and she continued, "You need to really ask yourself what you're fighting for and why you're fighting so hard for it. I understand that you feel an obligation toward your family, and I get it. But, if it costs you your personal life, that doesn't seem fair." Her head was shaking as her eyebrows pulled together. "You're willing to walk away from James because you've fallen into alignment with your dad's demands. He's ingrained it in your bones that it's either one or the other. But that's not true. And, even if it were, you'd really be okay with giving up James forever and pretending like he isn't the one person in the world who is meant for you?"

"Can I talk yet?" I whispered.

She cast me a harsh glare. "You've been scared to disappoint your dad your whole life. I see that so clearly now more than ever. But what about the fact that he's been disappointing you? If you continue to live your life for everyone else, then you're not living for yourself. I'm afraid you're going to look back at everything and hate yourself for it one day. Or at least have a huge ball of James Russo–sized regrets. At some point, you have to stop being worried about who you're letting down and realize that every time you go against your heart, you're letting yourself down. And that's way worse."

Silence hung in the air between us as I waited for more words to spill from her lips, so I could add them to the cyclone of thoughts currently spinning inside my mind.

When no more words came, she said, "Okay, you can talk now."

"I've never even thought about working for someone else before," I said, feeling a little stupid because it seemed like such a simple solution, if I were looking for one. I knew that almost any winery would hire me on the spot, but I'd never even considered that an option. I wasn't sure I wanted to. It was a big ask—to give up my legacy and what was supposed to be rightfully mine without a second thought.

"So, what are you thinking?" Jeanine's voice sounded hopeful for the first time since I'd arrived, but I knew that my response would change all that.

I sucked in an audible breath. "Honestly? I'm thinking that I don't know how to walk away from my family and still be okay with that. But I do know how to walk away from James. I've been doing it my whole life."

THE FIXER

James

MY PHONE RANG with a number that rarely ever called during my lifetime, but I had saved it nonetheless.

"Jeanine," I said into the speaker, wondering what exactly she was calling for.

"I need to talk to you, lover boy," she said.

I knew instantly that she was aware of what had gone down between me and Julia. I wasn't surprised or upset in the least, considering that she was Julia's best friend.

"I didn't do anything," I defended myself without any idea as to why, but once I started, I couldn't seem to stop. "I didn't hurt her, Jeanine. If anything, it's the other way around, so I'm not sure what exactly she told you, but ask her yourself."

"Jesus, Russo, shut up for one second and just meet me outside," she snipped and hung up.

I looked down at my phone just to make sure. Yep, she'd ended the call. Peering out one of the windows in the barn, I watched her impatiently pace back and forth, wondering why she was alone and where Julia was. Part of me wanted to see how long she'd wait before throwing a fit, but the other part was dying to know what she wanted to talk about.

I pulled open the heavy wooden door and walked into the season-changing air. It would grow colder soon, and we'd all be planning for next year's crops, myself included. Maybe this would be the year that I could actually give Julia a run for her money. Hell, maybe she'd even help me create a blend that was as good as hers. A guy could dream.

Jeanine's head whipped from side to side as she searched for me, clearly unaware of which direction I'd be coming from. Once she finally spotted me, she pushed off her car and stormed in my direction, stopping me dead in my tracks. I looked past her, for Julia's car, but didn't see it.

Jeanine's blonde hair blew around her face as she reached me, pushing a well-manicured fingernail against my chest.

"James"—her tone was instantly serious as she glanced around, clearly checking for someone or something—"can we go somewhere more private to talk?"

She looked nervous, and I started to grow nervous in response.

"Sure. Follow me." I led us back toward the barn, which was as empty as I'd just left it. "Do you want to sit?" I asked, feeling more and more uneasy by the second.

"No, I'm good." She looked around the barn before spotting my paintings and heading toward them, her head tilted appreciatively. "These are really good. Who painted them?"

"One of our staff," I lied. The last thing I wanted to talk about right now was my paintings. I wanted to know what she needed. "What's going on?"

Jeanine sucked in a long breath, her lips pressing tightly together as she stared at me for an uncomfortable amount of time. "Julia's dad kicked her out yesterday," she explained with a slight wince.

I felt like the wind had been knocked from my lungs.

"He kicked her out?" I couldn't believe it. I mean, I'd heard him threaten her. But to actually follow through? And for what? What had she even done? "Why did he do it? Because of me?"

"Yeah," she answered.

I reached for a lone barstool and pulled it under me as I practically fell on top of it.

"Where is she?" I wanted to race through the door, get into my car, and go find her. I could only imagine how upset she was, and I needed to be there for her even if she thought she didn't need me back.

"At my place."

"Is she okay? How is she?" I asked before feeling immensely stupid.

Of course she wasn't okay. How could she be?

"She's upset, James. Confused. Angry. Sad," Jeanine explained.

My heart fucking ached with every beat. I wanted to fix this for her, for her family, and for us.

"Is she mad at me? Why didn't she call me and tell me? Does she know you're telling me?"

Her head shook quickly. "She doesn't know I'm telling you. I tried to get her to call you last night, but she wouldn't do it. She's pretending like she doesn't have feelings for you so that this all hurts less."

"Yeah"—I cracked a slight smile—"she's good at that."

Jeanine turned overly defensive of her best friend, her back straightening as she cast me a glare. "Good at what exactly?" she questioned.

"Pretending like she doesn't like me," I said innocently.

Jeanine relaxed. "Well, you're not wrong about that."

"I know."

"Look, Julia didn't want to tell you, but I thought you should know. I thought you would want to know what was going on with her, especially after what happened between the two of you."

She offered me a sympathetic look, and I got up from the barstool and stood in front of her, my frame towering over hers.

"Thank you." I placed my hands on her shoulders before pulling her in for a hug. "I really appreciate you giving me a heads-up. I would have had no idea, and when I eventually found out, it would have killed me."

She pulled out of my grasp and squeezed my face. "I know. I figured as much. Now, do me a solid and fix this mess," she said before walking away and leaving me alone with my thoughts.

My mind had already been spinning with ways on how to make this right between Julia and her dad, but now that Jeanine had put the responsibility squarely on my shoulders, it almost felt too heavy to bear.

How could I possibly repair the damage when I was the one to cause it in the first place?

Shaking my head, I found myself growing angry. I wasn't the reason her dad had kicked her out. Sure, I might have been the scapegoat for it, but it really had nothing to do with me, and I refused to sit here any longer and take the blame. The feud between our families had gone on long enough, and I, for one, no longer wanted to participate in it. There couldn't be a war between two sides if one side wasn't fighting.

I knew what I needed to do. I just had no idea if I'd actually survive it.

I CONSIDERED TALKING to my parents first before heading into battle, but I pussed out. There was still a large part of me that had been so ingrained to stay away from the La Bellas that any pushback from my dad would have had me reconsidering my actions. I needed to do this while I still believed it was my only option.

Knocking hard on the La Bellas' front door, which I somehow knew had been handcrafted and flown in from Italy over a hundred years ago, I held my breath and waited. Maybe this wasn't the best idea. I probably should have told Dane that I was coming over here. That way, if my body went missing, they'd at least know where to start looking.

The door slowly pulled open—for dramatics or because of the sheer weight of it, I couldn't be sure. Behind it stood Mr. La Bella. His expression always looked like he'd bitten into a sour grape, and it turned even more sour upon seeing my face.

"What the hell do you want, boy? Your daddy send you over here to steal something?"

I was shocked into silence before I found my resolve. I would no longer be intimidated by this terrifying man. "I wanted to talk to you, sir."

He spat out a disgusted laugh. "I don't talk to Russos."

He moved to close the door, but I pressed my hand against it, stopping it cold.

"Mr. La Bella, please. I want to talk about Julia."

The door flew wide open as he stepped out, forcing me to take two awkward steps back. "Stay the hell away from my daughter!"

"With all due respect, sir, you did kick her out. I don't have to stay away from her now." I knew I was pushing the envelope, but it seemed like the only way to get through to the man or at least get him to see the reality of what he was doing.

"I kicked her out to teach her a lesson," he growled, closing the space between us.

I met his glaring, hard eyes with my own, refusing to back down. Not even when I heard Julia's mom gasp in shock so loud that it almost made me want to stop fighting. Clearly, she hadn't known what her husband had done to their only daughter, but putting an end to this feud mattered too much to me to stop now.

"What lesson is that exactly? That you don't care about her or what she's done for your winery? She's amazing, you know. The blends she creates and the passion she has for the science behind it. She's so fucking incredible, and you don't even see it. You take her for granted, and that's something I'd never do if I was lucky enough to have her," I promised as adrenaline took over my entire body, fueling the words to spill out without refrain. I would fight for her. Even if it meant going up against the man who had helped make her.

I was so wound up that I didn't notice that both of my parents had joined us outside until my dad said my name in an effort to get me to stop or attempt to regain some sense of composure.

Was I shouting? I wondered.

Ignoring his pleas, I continued addressing Mr. La Bella solely, "I'm just wondering what lesson she's supposed to be learning right now while she's crying at her best friend's apartment because she thinks her dad hates her. Maybe you were trying to show her that family is replaceable and that your only daughter means so little to you that you'd take everything from her the second she disobeyed you. Or that all that really matters is following decades-old rules that make no sense and don't even apply anymore. You're punishing her, and I don't think you even know why." I was definitely shouting now.

"James! That's enough." My dad's voice met my ears, and I turned to face him.

It was the first time I'd seen my parents and Julia's this close to one another without verbal taunts and assaults being launched back and forth.

"He's right," a soft voice spoke.

All eyes turned toward Mrs. La Bella. She placed her hands on her hips, her body still a good length away from her husband's.

"James is right. This feud was bound to eventually blow up in all of our faces. I've seen the way your son looks at my daughter. He's been doing it his whole life. It was only a matter of time before it all came crashing down around us."

"I agree," my mom spoke up.

And the two women turned toward one another without another word in some sort of womanly solidarity gesture that I swore only they could understand. We three men watched as they embraced in a hug like they had been lifelong friends instead of forced enemies, wondering what the hell had just happened and how in the world women could speak volumes to each other without using any words.

Mr. La Bella made a gargled sound like a wounded animal before speaking up, "So, we're all just going to pretend like we're okay with this? Like my daughter and your son being together doesn't go against everything both of our families stand for and represent? Our great-grandfathers are probably turning over in their graves right now, disgusted at what we've allowed to happen."

"They probably are," my dad agreed before adding, "but that doesn't mean we have to."

"What are you saying, Russo?" Mr. La Bella pointedly asked my dad.

I felt myself stand a little taller, wondering the same thing.

"I'm saying that maybe everyone who came before us was wrong." My dad blew out a breath, and I hid my surprise. It was the last thing I'd expected to hear him say. "It's exhausting, hating you. Aren't you tired?"

Now, that was a sentiment I could relate to.

"No," Mr. La Bella said with confidence.

I felt myself deflating like a balloon with a pinpricked hole in it.

Sucking in a quick breath that started to taste like defeat, I raised my hand into the air to get everyone's attention before speaking, "The hatred and the feud end with me. I'm not participating in it anymore, and I won't raise my future kids to either." Scanning the group, I noticed both of the moms smiling, and it gave me that little push of confidence to continue. "I mean it. And, if your daughter will have me, I plan on having those future kids with her, so you all can either get on board or live the rest of your lives without us in it."

It was a bold move, my speaking for both Julia and myself. And hell, for all I knew, I could be way off base. Julia might restart this feud simply based on what I'd just said. But my instincts told me otherwise. They told me that this was a fight worth fighting and that Julia wanted it just as badly as I did; she was just way too scared. She felt like she had too much to lose.

When no one argued or said a single word in response, I faced Mr. La Bella one last time. "Can I ask you one more thing?"

"Why stop now?" he responded coolly.

I nodded with a slight grin because I knew somewhere deep inside of me that I'd won this round.

"Do you even know about the bet? Like, what really happened between our families? And I'm only asking because I know for a fact that Julia doesn't. She doesn't even know half the story. So, I'm betting that you don't either."

"Is that true?" my dad questioned, his tone filled with disbelief. "You really don't know? How can you not know?"

Mr. La Bella's hands balled into fists before he released them. "Of course I know! You think I'd hate you for no reason? Your family tried to steal our vineyard out from under us. They told lies and bribed officials to take our land and put it in your name. Is that not the story you've been told all these years? Wouldn't surprise me if *we* were the villains in your version," he huffed.

"You're not wrong. That is part of it," I said with a nod. "But that's only part."

"What else could there be that even matters then?" Mr. La Bella asked gruffly.

My dad and I exchanged looks, both of our heads shaking because he didn't even know the half of it.

"Do you want to hear the whole thing or not?" my dad asked.

We all held our collective breath as we waited to hear what Mr. La Bella's answer would be.

CHOOSE RIGHT

Julia

JEANINE WALKED THROUGH her front door, and I practically attacked her.

"Finally."

I'd been home alone all day, so I'd slept more than I had in weeks, and I'd overly thought every single moment I'd ever had with James in my entire life at least three times before I decided to clean her house from top to bottom just to get my brain to shut up and stop spinning.

"Jesus, Julia." She looked around, her eyes wide. "You should stay here more often."

"I was bored." I plopped down onto the couch. "And you know I don't sit still well. I don't know how to do nothing."

"I can see that. Come be bored here anytime you want. It looks amazing."

"So, I take it, my dad didn't fire you since you were gone all day?" I practically whined.

She dropped her purse and keys on top of the kitchen counter before hopping up on it as well, putting her dirty shoes on top of the very surface I'd just scrubbed to a sparkle. I pretended not to care that she was defiling all my hard work.

"Nope. Not fired," she said with a sly smile.

I stopped thinking about the dirty surface and focused on the fact that she was up to something. The look on her face gave her away.

"What did you do?"

She feigned innocence. "Whatever do you mean?"

I managed a laugh as she fanned herself with her hand, pretending to be a Southern lady. But true Southern ladies would never put their dirty shoes on a countertop.

"Jeanine, tell me what you did." I leaned forward on the couch, tucking my legs up under me.

"I hate that I can't keep anything from you," she groaned. "Don't hate me, but I might have told James that your dad kicked you out," she admitted before wincing.

I squeezed my eyes shut for only a second or two. "Might have or did?"

"Definitely did."

"What did he say?"

"Mostly, he asked if you were okay. He was worried. It was really sweet. He really cares about you, you know," she said as if she were telling me something I didn't already know.

"I know he does." I did know. Or at least, I thought I did. I always thought I understood just how much I'd been denying my feelings for him my whole life, but I truly had no idea until the night I'd let myself fall into bed with him. Self-realization was a funny thing when you thought you were already pretty self-aware.

She hopped off the counter, and I wanted to shout in celebration while simultaneously wiping down where she'd just been perched. Instead, I stayed put as she made her way over to me, kicked off her shoes, and sat down.

Oh, sure, now, she took her shoes off.

"So"—she paused as she adjusted to get comfortable, causing my body to bounce on the cushions—"have you changed your mind yet?"

I gave her a confused look. "About what?"

"About James, dummy," she said like I was the stupidest person on the planet.

"What about him?" I needed her to clarify what she meant exactly.

"About giving up on him. Walking away from him. Have you decided to fight for the right thing yet?"

The right thing. Her accusation stung.

"I wish it were that easy."

She tsked me, her disappointment apparent. "It is that easy. You choose him over your brain-dead dad. You choose the guy who would stand beside you instead of the one who kicked you to the curb. You make a choice, Julia. And you choose James the same way he's so obviously chosen you."

To be honest, it was one of the topics I'd been thinking about all day. I'd been trying to figure out how to keep my family winery and be with James, too. Was it even possible? If I gave my dad an ultimatum, would he really disown me? And, if he did, would James's family even accept me, or would we both be ostracized from those we loved because we wanted to be together? How far would our families go to punish the two of us for having feelings for each other and wanting to see where this led?

"I don't know how to choose him. At least, not yet."

A small smile curved her lips as she asked, "But you want to?"

My heart kicked up a notch as I finally said the words out loud for the first time, "I do."

Three hard knocks at the front door made us both jump before our eyes locked on each other.

"Who is it?" I whisper-shouted.

Jeanine shrugged her shoulders. "How would I know?" she whisper-shouted back and moved to get up from the couch.

I tried to stop her, reaching for her arms but missing as she scooted away from my failing grasp. What if it was my dad? Or my mom? Neither one of them had called all day to check on me, and the realization caused my heart to ache. I had never felt more alone and abandoned than I did today.

"Don't answer it!" I demanded but had no real idea why.

"Why not, weirdo? It's my house." She shook her head and opened the front door with a laugh. "Well, well, well, speak of the devil."

I knew instantly that James had come. Jeanine pulled the door wide, allowing him to walk through before closing it behind him.

"As much as I want to stay here and witness this, I'll give you two some privacy," she said before walking into her bedroom and shutting the door loud enough for us both to hear.

Glancing down at my yoga pants and oversize T-shirt, I wished that I had dressed a little cuter. I wasn't even wearing a bra, not that I was sure James would mind that particular fact. Touching the messy bun on top of my head, I pulled a few strands loose so that they framed my face, making it look more like a cute, intentional hairstyle instead of a practical one for housecleaning.

"Stop fussing. You look perfect," James said, pulling my hand away from my hair.

I adjusted my head upward to look at him. I mean, really look at him. His blue eyes looked hopeful instead of sad, and that surprised me. I'd assumed that James would be feeling just as helpless as I felt, but he obviously wasn't, and for whatever reason, that pissed me off.

"What are you doing here?" I hadn't meant to bite his head off, but it'd definitely come out that way.

His body reacted as if I'd physically struck him, and I knew I should apologize, but I didn't.

"I came to take you home."

"Take me home? Are you insane? I can't go back there."

"You can," he said calmly as I sat there, feeling anything but calm.

"I can't."

"You can."

"Jesus, James, I just said, I can't. I know you know that my dad kicked me out. So, what game are you playing?"

"Can you stop arguing and listen to me for once in your damn life?" His voice rose, his cool facade now gone.

He was irritated, and it was because of me. But I was irritated now, and it was because of him. So, I guessed we were even.

"You think yelling at me will get me to listen to you?"

"I think yelling is the only way to get you to be quiet for ten seconds." He fought back, and I snapped my jaw shut in response. "See?"

"Why are you here?"

"I told you already. I came to get you. I came to bring you home."

Why was he doing this?

"I can't go with you, James. I'm not ready to face them. I need more time to figure out a plan."

He moved next to me on the couch. His hand reached for my thigh, his thumb drawing lazy circles on it. "Julia, I want to be with you. And not just for a week or a month or a year. I'm in this with you for the long haul. The forever kind if we're as good together as a couple as I think we will be. With that being said, I'm here to hold your hand. To stand by your side and go either force your dad to listen to reason or to help you walk away from him and decide what your next move is. It's entirely up to you, but whatever you decide, I'm doing it with you."

"You'd do all that for me?"

My eyes started to tear up, and James pressed his forehead against mine.

"I'd do anything for you," he breathed out, and I knew he meant it.

"My dad will probably shoot us both on the spot," I said, trying to be funny, but even I wasn't sure how untrue that statement was.

"He won't," James tried to reassure me.

He sounded so convincing, so sure of himself, but I couldn't believe it.

"How do you know that?" I asked.

James pulled back, his hand now on my cheek as his blue eyes stared a hole right through me. He moved slowly forward, his lips pressing against mine, and I didn't fall into the kiss. I dived in, headfirst, with every part of me. His tongue brushed my lip before touching my own, and chills raced through my body. I forgot who I was, who James was, and what we were supposed to be as our mouths opened and closed in unison, the heat between us growing like a wildfire. When James broke the kiss, a small whimper escaped me, and I looked at him, half-mortified at my desire for him, but he smiled, his face completely flushed.

"Do you trust me, babe?" It was a loaded question, and he knew it. It was also the first time he'd called me any endearing name, and my heart danced inside my chest in response to hearing it. It liked the nickname.

The answer came to me without thinking. It wasn't something I needed to contemplate even though, if he had asked me a month ago, I would have said the exact opposite, convinced that trusting him would be something I could never do.

"Yes," I said.

And his face lit up like I'd just promised him all of my future wine recipes and the south side vines.

THAT DAMN BET

James

"THEN, LET'S GO." I pushed up from the couch and extended my hand, waiting for Julia to take it. I knew she would. I just knew.

And, when she finally did, interlacing her fingers with mine, all the pieces of my cracked heart pulled themselves back together.

I glanced back, noticing Jeanine peeking out from her bedroom door, and gave her a reassuring wink. She gave me a thumbs-up. I pulled Julia outside, down the stairs, and toward my waiting car. We'd come back for her things later. Julia wouldn't be staying here anymore, and I knew it. She was the only one who didn't.

The drive back to her place was quiet, much like our first date. I waited for her to ask me a million questions, but when they never came, I stayed silent and gave her space. But I never pulled my hand from hers. And, each time I glanced over at her sitting in my passenger seat, she was already watching me with those big doe hazel eyes that I loved.

We belonged together. I'd always known it, but nothing solidified it more than seeing her sitting next to me in my car. She couldn't hide the way she felt about me either. Not anymore. Not even if she tried. My girl was the walking heart-eyed emoji come to life. Of course, I'd never tell her that because I didn't want it to stop, and purely out of spite, Julia would definitely try to be another emoji if she knew.

When we pulled onto our properties and I maneuvered my car toward her side instead of mine, her breathing escalated.

"What are you doing?" she asked nervously as she tried to yank her hand from my grasp, but I only gripped it tighter.

"Calm down. It's okay," I said before releasing her, so we could both get out of the car.

I hopped out as quickly as I could and made my way toward her side of the car, but she had already gotten out. I trapped her there, pressing her body against the cold metal as I stood in front of her, blocking her path.

My hands snaked down the curves of her waist before landing on her hips and holding on tight. She opened her mouth to say something, and I took the words from her, my lips pressing against hers as my tongue moved inside, making her moan. Her body simultaneously relaxed and tightened as her hips started softly grinding against me. I didn't think she even realized she was doing it, but I noticed every single way her body reacted to my touch.

Breaking the kiss, I took her hand in mine once more in a show of solidarity. We were walking into the La Bella home the same way we'd be leaving it—together.

"Do you think this might make it worse?" She nodded toward our hands as her eyes nervously started to well up with tears.

I stopped walking to wipe them away before tilting her head up by the chin. "I would never do anything to hurt you. Now, don't let go," I said as I gave her a reassuring squeeze. I moved to open her front door without knocking. "Damn, this thing's heavy."

Her lips quirked upward but didn't fully form a smile before her entire expression changed into a mixture of confusion and shock and surprise. "What ..." she stumbled over her words as her eyes fixated on her kitchen table and all four of our parents sitting around it.

Instead of killing one another or shouting like usual, they were laughing and drinking our respective wines.

It was almost like they were old friends.

If old friends threatened each other on a daily basis and forbade their children from being friends.

"What's going on?" she whispered to me. "Why aren't they at each other's throats?"

"You'll see." I kissed the side of her head in front of everyone because I wanted them all, Julia included, to know how serious I was about her and about us.

"Julia, sit," her dad instructed, but his tone was softer than I'd ever heard before.

She looked around the table before reluctantly sitting down at the chair I'd pulled out for her. I moved to sit right next to her and reached for her hand under the table.

Her mom leaned toward her and whispered loud enough for me to hear, "I didn't know he kicked you out, honey. I had no idea until I heard it from James."

"Heard it from James?" Julia looked at me before shaking her head like she had no idea what on earth could have transpired in the last twenty-four hours to shake up our entire world. "Hello, Mr. and Mrs. Russo. It's, uh," she stumbled, "nice to see you in our home, I think."

My parents laughed and greeted her back before sipping more of her latest award-winning wine.

"This is really good, sweetheart. You're very talented." My mom complimented her latest creation.

"Thank you so much. So, what is everyone doing here?" she asked, still nervous and completely unsettled.

"We were waiting for you," her mom answered with a smile before pouring her and me a glass of wine.

"Why me? What for?" Julia nervously looked around. "Oh my God, is this an intervention or something? Are you sending me away?"

The table erupted with laughter.

"We were waiting for you, so we could all hear the story at the same time," her dad announced over the chaos.

"What story?"

I looked her in the eyes before responding, "About our great-grandfathers and this stupid bet."

Her eyes grew wide, and I watched her swallow hard. "Oh. I've always wanted to hear this." She sat up straighter, her attention solely focused on me.

"We ready?" I asked, mostly waiting for the okay from Julia's dad to start.

He took a large gulp of my second-place wine and nodded, giving me the go-ahead.

I wasn't sure where to start, so I started from the beginning. "Okay. Well, as you might or might not know, our great-grandfathers really liked to gamble with each other and the other townsfolk. Aside from getting into trouble at the local bar, there wasn't much else to do back then, so that's what they tended to do. Our great-grandfathers had been best friends since childhood, you know?"

There was a mixture of grumbling at the table, and I realized that Mr. La Bella didn't even know this part, so I continued, "They immigrated here together from Italy. Their dream was to buy land next to each other in America and start wineries like the ones they'd had in Italy. They were ecstatic when they found this area and were able to make their dreams come true. They never thought they'd stop being friends." I looked around the table. "Did you know that part?"

"I didn't," Mr. La Bella answered in a seemingly shocked tone that surprised me.

"How could your family leave out all the important details?" my dad asked.

"I have no idea. And I never questioned it because I was perfectly fine with hating you for the reasons I had been given," was all he said in response.

I continued the story, "Okay, so they were best friends, but like any good rivalry between men, there was a woman." I raised my eyebrows, and Julia offered me a sad sort of smile. "I guess they both fell in love with the same girl. *My* great-grandmother."

Julia interrupted, "So, your great-grandfather got the girl, and that's why our families hate each other?"

I shook my head. "You'd have the answer if you let me finish telling the story."

"My bad," she said with a little extra snark and a little less apology.

She wasn't sorry at all, but I'd punish her for that later. When no one else was around.

"So, yes, my great-grandfather got the girl, and, yes, your great-grandfather was bitter about it. He apparently stayed single for a long time, living next door to his best friend and the girl he thought should have been his. One night, during one of their poker games, my great-grandfather was complaining about the land on the south side."

Everyone seemed to subconsciously lean in a little closer to me, and I knew I had their full attention. It was as if they sensed what had started the whole rivalry in the first place was about to be revealed.

"The land on the south side—as you well know, seeing as how it's your land now—is a little bit of a pain in the ass. The way the land slopes and curves, not to mention that steep drop-off down the side, well, my great-grandfather had a hard time figuring out how to effectively manage it. He was really struggling with it."

"I can't imagine trying to maintain it back then without all the innovation we have now," Julia said, her eyes wide as she sipped her own glass of wine.

"Anyway, he was complaining about it, and your great-grandfather said he'd take it off his hands. I think he was joking, but things quickly turned serious. They were always betting—one or the other losing money one night and getting it back the next. My great-grandfather put that particular plot of land on the table after one too many drinks."

Julia's jaw dropped open, and I knew that she could tell what was coming next, but I said it anyway, "He lost the land, and that night, when he told my great-grandmother what he'd done, she insisted he march right back over and get it back. But your great-grandfather said that a wager was a wager, and he had won it fair and square."

"He's not wrong," Mr. La Bella said with a shrug, and all eyes fell to him. "I'm just saying, if you bet and lose, you don't get to take it back. That's not the way betting works. If you're going to be a man and bet manly things, you have to be willing to part with them."

"Son, please continue," my dad instructed.

"In the weeks that followed, my great-grandfather kept trying to get yours to bet the land again, so he could have a shot at winning it back, but yours refused to play for it. Apparently, he'd already gone to the courthouse to put the new land markings in writing, so the land was legally his, pending the new deed. My great-grandfather eventually backed down, but their relationship was never the same after that. I think it could have been repaired at some point, if it wasn't for the fact that—" I started to explain when Julia interrupted me.

"Wait. The south side vines were originally yours?" She sounded so surprised and a little sad, like I'd just ripped a dream from her grasp or changed it somehow.

"They were. But no one knew what those vines would produce at the time."

"So, if they didn't know, then why did your great-grandfather want it back so bad? Why was he that pissed to lose it?"

"I think because my great-grandmother asked him to. She was really disappointed and angry with him when she found out what he'd done. It was like she knew that it would cause a further rift between them, and she had felt guilty enough as it was for coming between their lifelong friendship. She always warned my great-grandfather not to gamble cars, homes, or land. She insisted that they were too personal and that people got too angry and couldn't forgive that kind of loss."

Julia nodded, and then I dealt the final blow, "Once the south side vines started producing its one-of-a-kind grapes, that soured what little had been left between them to nothing."

"Is that the end?" Julia asked.

I looked around the table, nodding before finishing off my own glass of wine.

"What about the parts that I was told, growing up? You didn't even mention those," Mr. La Bella asked, his brow furrowed as if he wasn't sure which direction was up anymore.

My dad took over, and I was grateful. "After the bet, like James mentioned, my grandfather kept trying to get the land back. He did more than just try to play for it again in poker. He asked your grandfather to split it in half. Then, he offered to buy it back for double what it was worth and then triple, but your grandfather kept saying no. I think it was in part just to torture him. I'm sure your grandfather couldn't have cared less about the vines, especially since he didn't even know what they would come to produce at that point."

Mr. La Bella sat there, taking it all in, his head shaking back and forth in disbelief. I squeezed Julia's hand under the table, and she squeezed it back. The gesture made me smile as my dad wrapped the rest of the story up.

"My grandfather's insistence on there being some way to get the land back only fueled your grandfather's stubbornness to keep it. To be honest, I think he liked having something over my great-grandfather, especially since he felt like my great-grandfather had something over him," he said, referring to my great-grandmother. "But, once the land started producing grapes that didn't taste like any other in the county, all hell broke loose. My great-grandfather went to the courts and tried to fight to get the land deed overturned, but they refused, saying too much time had passed. He told anyone who would listen that your grandfather had stolen the land from him and was crooked. He even called the police, but nothing worked. The bitterness grew between our families because Great-grandfather Russo refused to let it go, and Great-grandfather La Bella didn't take kindly to being called a thief and a liar."

"That's the only part of the story I've ever known." Mr. La Bella slowly shook his head, as if still in disbelief. "You're sure it's accurate? You're not just selling me some bullshit right now?"

"To what end?" my dad questioned. "No, really? We're not asking for the land back, so why would we lie to you?"

"It sounds plausible though, don't you think, dear?" Julia's mom asked her husband, and it didn't escape me that he failed to respond.

"I will say this just for the record," my mom piped up, her tone serious. "I've heard this story at least a hundred times since I met my husband. And it's never changed once. Not a single detail. And I heard it from both his grandfather before he passed and his father." She looked at my dad with a soft smile. "I just think that if it was a lie, something in the story would have changed by now."

"I agree with that," Julia added. "Can I ask something?"

We all focused our attention on her and waited.

"Can we stop hating each other now? Can we be done with it? I really want to be done with it," she pleaded, as if somehow the story had just made things worse between our families instead of making them better.

A hearty laugh escaped my throat. "I've been done with it."

I looked deep into her hazel eyes and leaned forward, my lips pressing against hers, present company be damned. She tried to pull away, but my hand was on her neck, holding her tight.

Her dad cleared his throat, and only then did I break the kiss, still a little scared of him, to be honest.

"I want to make a toast." He reached for his empty wine glass and held it into the air before his wife pulled his arm down.

"Let's fill our glasses first," she suggested with a smile and a bottle of wine in hand.

Mrs. La Bella went to work, filling all six of our glasses. Each member of the Russo family got Julia's latest creation, and each member of the La Bella family got mine.

Once our glasses were filled, we held them in the air between us. The scene was something I'd never thought I'd witness in my lifetime, but I had always hoped for it. There was peace between the Russo and La Bella families. And I was determined to make it last.

OVERDUE APOLOGIES

Julia

MY DAD CLEARED his throat once more, and I held my breath in anticipation, my wine glass in front of me with all the others. What if he didn't believe the story and wanted to continue this pointless feud? My dad had never really been the forgiving type.

"First of all, I want to thank you for sharing that story. I've never heard it before, and I feel like an idiot for only learning about it now, after all this time. I've been so angry for so long."

My dad actually sounded vulnerable, and I realized that I'd never seen him that way in my entire life. He'd always been my dad, this mountain of a man who rarely showed any emotion and was tough as nails. He seemed like anything but in this moment. It was humbling and unnerving to see a parent's human side.

"I want to apologize to both my daughter and your son." He winced a little before continuing, and I knew swallowing his pride wasn't something that came naturally to him. "I knew you had feelings for her. I've always known. And I knew she had feelings for you back," he confessed.

I felt my cheeks heat with embarrassment. It was true, but being put on the spot like that in front of everyone was more than a little uncomfortable. The night was already overwhelming enough without adding this to the mix.

"That is why I behaved the way I did when it came to the two of you. It never occurred to me that I didn't know what had really happened between our two families. I always assumed I knew enough."

I moved to say something, but my dad stopped me, his gray eyes meeting mine. "Let me finish, Julia, please, or I'll never get it out."

I couldn't argue with that logic, so I stayed quiet and let him continue, "I'm not going to be perfect because hating you is as ingrained in my blood as this wine we're drinking." Everyone laughed a little in response. "I was raised to do it my whole life. But James was right earlier when he said it was time to stop, so I promise to do my best."

The part about James piqued my interest, and I wondered exactly what he meant. I'd make sure to ask him about it later.

"So, I'd like to make a toast. To new beginnings. To burying the old hatchet we should have never been asked to carry in the first place. And to our kids. Who are either going to burn our respective wineries to the ground or make them better than we ever could."

I frowned a little until everyone shouted, "Cheers!" in unison, and our six wine glasses clanked against one another.

I forcefully squeezed James's hand, and when he squeezed back so hard in return that it actually hurt, I was thankful for the pain. It meant that I was awake, and this crazy scene playing out in front of me was real and not a dream.

Molecules must have exploded all around us, breaking into a billion unseen pieces, leaving nothing but light in their wake as the decades-old hatred died on the spot. It was the only explanation for the way the air had instantly changed. I sucked in a long, deep breath, questioning if I'd ever breathed so easily in my entire life.

"I feel different," I said in a whisper, but everyone heard me, so it must have been louder than I'd realized.

"In a good way?" James asked, his eyes solely focused on mine.

I nodded. "Lighter. Looser. Freer?" I said it like a question, wondering if it was only me who was reacting this way to our newly found truce.

James smiled, a devilish grin that made me want to press my mouth against his, but I refrained. "I feel the same way. I feel relieved, and I never knew that I hadn't. Does that make any sense?"

"Completely," I reassured him, realizing that I didn't want him to feel alone or isolated in his feelings. How he felt mattered to me.

"It's a wonder the vines produced any grapes at all, what with all that negative energy we carried around." It was James's mom who said it, and the sentiment hit me square in the chest with all its rightness.

"Maybe, now, they'll be even better," I said with a smile as a world of possibilities felt like it had just opened up and was shining down on me.

Now that James and I were allowed to be together, I couldn't stop thinking about all the things we could do and try. I knew I was getting ahead of myself, but I didn't care. I'd work out the details later. Maybe while James was inside me.

He wouldn't be able to argue then, I thought to myself as a giggle escaped.

"What are you laughing at?" James asked and I felt my cheeks heat.

I knew I was blushing. "Nothing. Tell you later," I lied because I had absolutely no intention on telling James my dirty little secret.

James's mom yawned, which forced me to follow suit, and before I knew it, every one of us was doing it, our hands placed over our mouths as we giggled, and my ears popped.

"I think we should call it a night. I don't know about the rest of you, but forgiving you all is hard work. I'm exhausted," my dad said with a genuine smile as he made his way over toward Mr. Russo, and they shook hands.

It was the first time I'd ever seen them do that.

I smiled to myself. Tonight had been filled with so many firsts; it felt like a rebirth of sorts. It represented the beginning of everything to come and I was simultaneously excited and beat. Going through that kind of emotional upheaval, even when it was the best kind, wore you out. I felt like I could hit my mattress and sleep for a week.

"Do you want me to take you to get your car and your things from Jeanine's?" James asked, one hand in his pocket.

I looked around at my parents, who were both intently watching us, before I opted out. "Not tonight, but thank you. I want to talk to my parents a little more."

"Okay. What a night, right?" James said before giving me a soft kiss on the cheek. "Text me later?"

"I don't have your number," I teased, but it made him skip a step as soon as he started to walk out. He looked back at me, and I said, "Kidding."

"Text me, or I'll punish you later," he whispered into my ear.

I swatted him away, my eyes narrowing with all the words I wanted to say but couldn't. At least, not in front of my parents.

"Good night, Mr. and Mrs. La Bella," he bellowed from the front door as he disappeared behind his parents.

"Night, James," they said in response, my father's voice less enthusiastic than my mom's.

I turned to face them both. "You're not going to be mean again, are you?" I directed the question toward my dad.

"I'm going to try my damnedest, but that's a hard habit to break."

I knew he was talking about me and James being together. But this was something I was willing to fight for now. Once being with James had become an actual option, something we could both have without causing our parents to kill one another, I realized just how badly and deeply I wanted the chance to be with him. There would be no giving up on us now. I refused to go down without a damn good fight, and I braced myself for it, assuming that it was about to come even though my dad had just been cordial as hell.

My mom interjected, "Your father will absolutely behave himself and be on his best behavior from this night forward. Won't you, dear?"

He looked down at the woman he'd been married to for over thirty years and grimaced only slightly as he responded, "I'm going to try."

"Uh-uh." My mom shook her head with disapproval. "You're going to do more than try."

My dad swallowed hard, and I watched the lump in his throat move up and down. "I'll be nice," he slid out under his breath.

My mom patted his arm like he was a good boy. "Didn't you have something you wanted to say to Julia?" She continued to direct the conversation, and I felt like I was in an episode of *The Twilight Zone* where everything was a little backward and roles had reversed.

"I'm sorry I kicked you out. I was wrong to do that. Even with or without what happened tonight, I should have never done that to you. I was just so mad; I couldn't see straight." He tugged at his salt-and-pepper hair, the distress written all over his tired eyes.

"I know." I started to add that it was okay but stopped myself because it wasn't, and I didn't want to excuse his behavior.

"I think I was mostly mad because I had known it was coming. I had seen that storm brewing in the distance years ago, and I knew, once you crossed that line, there'd be no going back for either of you. I knew I wouldn't be able to keep you two away from each other, no matter what I did. Can you ever forgive me for trying?"

My eyes watered with my dad's admission. "If you can forgive the Russos, Dad, I'm willing to forgive just about anything," I said and meant it, my heart feeling so full that I thought it might burst inside my chest and flood my entire body. Ten more seconds, and I'd drown in a sea of my heart's own emotions.

Thankfully, the words stopped, and I hugged each of my parents before heading outside. I cast a quick glance at the Russo house and noticed that all the lights were still on. I wondered if they were discussing the evening more, like we had been, or if they were still celebrating.

My legs begged me to cross the imaginary line that no longer existed and knock on their front door for the first time in my life, but my mind stopped me. It was too tired for more words or feelings tonight, and so I trudged toward my tiny bungalow instead, a hot shower and my bed not only calling my name, but also screaming it.

Poor Jeanine had been texting me all night, threatening my life if I didn't at least give her a thumbs-up or down emoji. She informed me that she couldn't sleep until she knew something, ANYTHING—she had written in all caps.

I sent her a quick response with a thumbs-up to calm her nerves and told her I'd fill her in on everything tomorrow. My best friend was going to lose her mind over what had happened here tonight. And that would make two of us.

SPREADING RUMORS

James

MY PARENTS AND I stood around our butcher block table, each of us nursing the last bit of wine in our respective glasses as I checked my phone for at least the hundredth time since we'd gotten back from the La Bellas'. I wondered when and *if* Julia was ever going to text me like I'd asked. My mother teased me after the tenth time she caught me checking, and I had nothing to say for myself, except that I was a determined man who was currently obsessed with all things Julia La Bella. I had it bad.

"She'll call you," she tried to reassure me, but I wasn't convinced.

"I asked her to text when she got home. What if her dad changed his mind and told her to stay away from me again? He wouldn't do that, right?" I glanced between my parents, who looked more relaxed than I'd ever seen them before, their shoulders no longer tense, their faces no longer creased with worry lines.

My dad spoke up, "He won't change his mind. He can't. Not now that he knows the truth. And I saw the weight lift off of his body the same way it lifted from mine. Can't imagine he wants to go back to carrying it again. I sure as hell don't." He blew out a relieved breath, and it shocked me how much stress we'd all been forced to live with without truly realizing the physical effects.

I almost asked my parents if they were okay with the idea of Julia and me being together, but I didn't. Their blessing would make things easier, but I honestly didn't give a shit anymore. Nothing and no one was going to stop me from getting the girl. Not this time. Not ever again. And I decided that if Julia didn't send me a text within the next thirty minutes, I'd go over to her house and punish her just like I'd promised.

Hell, maybe that was exactly what she wanted. I wouldn't put it past my girl to push my buttons for fun. No sooner were the thoughts crossing my mind than my phone vibrated across the table, alerting everyone to the fact that I had a text message. I reached for it like it was a fire I needed to put out, a huge smile plastering itself on my face without my consent as soon as I noticed the sender's name on the screen. It was the name I'd had for her in my phone since we were teenagers even though I'd only seen it come across my screen once before—Julia LBR.

Here's your text, bossy.

I laughed out loud when I read her message, and my parents both looked at me with the dopiest expressions on their faces.

"What?" I tried to sound tough, but it was really hard to sound like a badass when you sported a giant smile you couldn't control.

"Go get the damn girl already," my dad encouraged, and he didn't need to tell me twice.

I bolted out the front door and jogged over to Julia's place, uninvited. I figured I'd beg for forgiveness from between her thighs if I had to, but I had a feeling she wouldn't be too pissed at me for showing up, unannounced.

Knocking on her door when all I wanted to do was kick it down and have my way with her took more restraint than I possessed in that moment. I stood there, my arms pinned on either side of the wood frame as I waited impatiently for it to open.

The second it did and I saw her surprised face, I reached for her like she was the only air I needed and crashed my lips against hers, throwing the door open in my wake and moving us both deeper inside. She opened easily, her tongue finding mine without hesitation, as our mutual lust filled the space between us. I reached for her ass, squeezing it, and she hopped up. When her legs wrapped around my waist, I almost died on the spot.

"God, this is so much better than fake hating you," she breathed out, her lips still pressed against mine as her eyes fluttered between open and closed.

I lowered her feet to the floor and held on to the back of her neck to keep her close. The last thing I wanted was her getting away from me before I was ready.

I continued to lick her lips, teasing her with my tongue before diving back inside her hot mouth. We moved in unison, our kisses as easy and natural as the sun rising and setting each day. It was like we'd been doing it our whole lives. I knew it was because she had been made for me, her lips the exact replica of what mine craved.

"We've wasted so much time being apart when we should have always been together."

She slightly pulled away, my hand dropping from her neck to let her, as her hazel eyes softened with my admission. "You really believe that about us?"

She moved backward to her couch and sat on the edge as my body instinctively followed hers. I stood between her open legs, her thighs pressing against my legs, holding me in place.

"What? That you never stood a chance with someone who wasn't me? Hell yes. It's the truth," I answered, steadfast in my feelings. I meant it. I believed it. And nothing would have ever changed my mind about it.

"And what about you?" Her smile was a little wicked as she toyed with me, but I knew she needed to hear me say it out loud, the same way I needed to hear the same admission from her.

No matter how strong either of us were, our vulnerability for each other lay right below the surface, two land mines just waiting to explode.

"Any other woman would have just been my version of a poor man's Julia. A second-place trophy. A mere replica because I couldn't have the original. And, deep down, I would have always known it and fucking hated it."

Her jaw slacked with her surprise. It seemed like I was always shocking her with my words, but it wasn't like it was the first time I'd admitted to having feelings for her.

"You know, you might have said all these things to me years ago and saved us both a little time," she answered like a smart-ass, her hands rubbing the sides of my legs as she looked up at me, her eyelashes batting.

"Uh, I tried to do that, remember? That time in the vineyard when I told you I wanted to be with you, and you smashed my heart into a million pieces," I said, bringing up one of the most painful memories of my young adult life.

Her eyebrows pulled together, and she looked distraught. "What are you talking about?"

I took a step back to not only break our physical contact, but to also look at her from a distance instead of so up close. "Um, that night in the vineyard. In high school?" I said it like a question because her confused expression hadn't lessened.

"I have no idea what you're talking about," she said, her full lips pursing like she'd eaten something rotten.

"You're joking, right? Messing with me?" I cocked a lopsided grin, but she shook her head.

"No. James, I honestly don't know what you're talking about. What night in the vineyard? Was this before or after you started that rumor?"

"You really don't remember?" I asked as the pieces started to fall into place.

She hadn't treated me any differently after that night, like I'd mistakenly thought. She didn't even remember it. Hell, my ego had been so damaged that I'd read into everything she didn't say in ways she never meant.

"Tell me, what happened?"

"It was the night you went out to drink all the wine. You were alone. Except for the four bottles by your side," I started to explain as her expression shifted, her eyebrows shooting up and her hand covering her mouth.

"Oh my God. You were there. I remember now that you showed up, and I was so pissed about you being there. But I don't remember anything after that."

I crossed the divide I'd created, moving my body back in between hers, and relaxed the second her hands found my sides again and started moving up and down.

"I spilled my heart to you that night. Told you that I had feelings for you and that I wanted to be with you. You told me that I didn't know what feelings were and that you'd never want to be with me. I even asked you again just to make sure. You were pretty adamant about your disgust for me."

"James"—she looked like someone had just punched her in the heart—"I woke up in the vineyard the next morning, and I could barely remember going out there in the first place. The empty wine bottles were scattered at my feet, and I threw up the second I tried to stand. That night has always been a complete blur to me."

"This whole time, I thought you remembered."

"Is that why you started the rumor?"

I shook my head because that hadn't been why at all. "You broke my heart that night, but the rumor was an accident," I started to explain.

She scoffed, "How could what you said be an accident? You told everyone I'd slept with you!"

"Because I was in love with you, Julia. Why did you think I'd started it?" Clearing the air and healing old wounds was cathartic even if it hurt to relive it in the moment.

Her hands moved from the sides of my legs to my waist, and I tried to focus on her words and not the touch of her fingertips sending sensations throughout my entire body.

"I thought you were trying to ruin my life. Like hating me wasn't enough for you, and you had to take it one step further."

"I never hated you."

"I know that now, but I didn't then." She swatted at me before faking a pout.

The rumor really hadn't been intentional on my part even though I'd been so bitter about her rejection that it probably looked that way from her perspective. Or at least, it would have, if she had remembered rejecting me in the first place.

"I overheard a few of my basketball teammates talking about you in the locker room one afternoon after practice, and I lost my shit," I started to tell her the story as my mind flashed back.

"Hey, Russo. What do you think Julia would say if I asked her out?" my teammate Todd Lestare shouted.

I slung a towel around my shoulder as I opened my locker. "I have no idea. Why do you want to? She's not even remotely your type," I said, hoping he would take offense and back the hell off.

Todd usually liked girls who were a little less difficult, and the thought of him anywhere near Julia made my skin crawl.

"Maybe it's time to branch out," he said.

My hands balled into fists at my sides. "Running out of options?" I practically growled.

He laughed like it was the most absurd question on the planet. "Yeah, right, Russo. I don't run out of options. Is it wrong that I want to be the one who takes the La Bella princess's virginity? Think of it as a merger," he said through a sly grin.

It took everything in me not to sock him in the fucking jaw as another teammate gave him a high five. I wanted to high five his face. With a chair.

"Well, I hate to be the one to break it to you, but you're too late for that title." The words were out of my mouth before I could stop them.

Dane suddenly appeared at my side and whispered harshly, "What are you doing?"

"Just go with it." I gave him a hard look, and he shook his head.

"No way! Who'd she give it up to?"

I shrugged my shoulders, not wanting to say the words out loud since they were a blatant lie, but knowing that I would if that was what it took to keep him away from her.

Thankfully, I didn't have to answer.

Dane stepped up, answering for me, "Come on, Lestare. A gentleman never tells."

"You? Dane?" Todd looked at him in disbelief. "No fucking way."

"No, not me," Dane shot him an incredulous look as he gave a slight nod in my direction.

"Who then?" Todd looked between the two of us. "Russo? My man!" he shouted before raising his hand in the air and waiting for me to slap it.

I begrudgingly obliged, but that single gesture confirmed his guess and solidified the lie. It might be a shit thing to do, but I was convinced that I was doing the right thing by her. Todd Lestare would have taken something precious from her that he couldn't give back, and he would have made sure everyone in town knew it'd happened. He would have humiliated her. And I had no idea I was about to do the same thing.

"But, wait, I thought you two hated each other?" another player asked.

"Yeah, well, sometimes, the hate makes it better," I said, adding to the lie.

"Care if I ask her out? Take her for a spin?" Todd asked like Julia was a fucking car everyone was entitled to drive.

"Like hell," I bit out in response before circling to face all of my teammates, who were suddenly all ears. "None of you assholes had better touch her or even think about asking her out. You hear me? She's off-limits. If I hear otherwise, we'll have a big fucking problem."

"Never pegged you for the jealous type, Russo," Todd added before placing a hand on my shoulder.

I tossed it off. "Stay away from her."

Her eyes were as wide as saucers. "Todd? Oh my God. No wonder you hated that I'd agreed to go to dinner with him!"

"I would have hated it anyway, but it made it worse that it was him of all people." I swallowed the anger rising in my throat as I reminded myself that I'd gotten the girl.

I got the girl.

I got the girl.

"I can't believe that's how it started. I had no idea, and of course, I just assumed the worst," she said with a shrug.

"You know, that you were a total lying asshole who wanted to ruin me for all others."

I felt a little stupid and immature, but I also knew that I'd do it all over again if I had to. "It killed me the day you told me to take it back. I knew that I couldn't do it. I couldn't bear the thought of anyone on my team touching you, let alone taking the one thing I thought I'd never get to have."

"Surprise, Russo, you've had it." She laughed and waved an arm in the air like a game show hostess. "And, just for the record, I was never interested in Todd Lestare."

I swallowed hard. "Good. Because the thought of you with him makes me want to stab my own eyes out, so I don't have to see it in my head."

"Little dramatic, don't you think?" she asked through a soft giggle, but I could tell she was enjoying the jealous side of me.

I wasn't proud of it, but sometimes, feelings weren't in our control. And, when it came to Julia La Bella, my resolve was only so strong, my emotions only so in check.

"Not when it comes to you. Not when it comes to us."

"There's an us now? Is this official?"

"There's always been an us, Julia. You were just too stubborn or scared to admit it. Tell me you've always wanted me."

She stayed quiet, purely to torture me I was sure.

"Julia," I ground out, my knee moving to press against her core.

Her body writhed in response. "Fine. You know I have."

"But I've never heard you say it." My knee moved in small, torturous circles, causing her mouth to open and her tongue to peek out.

"I'm saying it now." She sounded breathy.

"Say it with actual words."

"I've always wanted you, James. Everyone knows it. Everyone but you apparently."

Her eyes shot up to meet mine and held them there. My knee stopped moving. I thought my heart had stopped beating. My mind definitely short-circuited before it switched back on. I reached down and scooped her body from the couch as she squealed in half-shock, half-delight.

"Where are you taking me?" she asked through a smile.

"To bed, where you belong." I easily moved through her tiny house, knowing exactly where I was headed this time.

"Am I being punished?" She batted those damn lashes at me, and I almost stopped in the hallway and fell to my knees. I didn't need a bed for what I planned on doing to her.

"I plan on punishing you all night. First, with my tongue. Then, with my dick. Think you can handle it?" My inner caveman had come out to play, and the smile on her face told me everything I needed to know. Not only could she handle it, but my girl also couldn't wait for it.

COUPLE GOALS

Julia

I'D LEARNED THE first time that James Russo was a god in the sack, but it'd still held true the second time. And the third. And the fourth. And, currently, as he was under the covers, between my thighs, doing all the things I'd always dreamed about with that beard and tongue.

I tangled a hand in his dark hair, the morning light spilling through my curtains as I raked my nails along his back with my other. It was too much, the way he so skillfully licked me, sending me over the edge time and time again, reading me like a treasure map he'd been given the key to.

"James, please," I begged.

I'd learned pretty quickly that he liked it when I begged for him to stop eating me out and get inside me.

"Please what?" His breath was hot against my core as I tossed the sheets off to look at him. His hair was ruffled and messed up from my hands moving through them.

"Please get inside me. I want you in me. Why do you make me beg for it?"

He licked his lips and wiped at his beard with one hand before slowly sliding up my body, never breaking contact. The sensation of his warm skin pressing against mine was almost enough to send another orgasm erupting through me. James and I were definitely connected and in more than just the physical way. Anyone could connect with someone on that level.

There was something bigger and deeper at play here. The cord that bonded us was on full display even if it couldn't be seen. We both felt it, tugging and tightening around our bodies, as if to make it known that there would be no more untethering after this. I couldn't imagine wanting to untangle myself from James ever again anyway, so I silently willed the bond to strengthen. I wouldn't fight it anymore. There would be no more opposition from this end.

I had officially surrendered.

James pressed his tip against my core, and he slowly moved inside me.

"You're doing that on purpose," I said, unable to catch my breath.

"Yep," was all he said in response.

I could tell that it was taking him a tremendous amount of restraint to not plunge in me all at once, but when James set his mind to something, he achieved it. Aside from beating me in competitions, of course.

He pulled out before pushing back in, getting a little deeper with each thrust until he was finally all the way inside. Then, he stopped moving altogether, the full length and width of him filling me completely as we shared the same air, our eyes locked. I started to wiggle my hips, but he pinned me with his gaze before asking me to stop, and once again, I submitted without complaint.

When James finally started moving again, I wanted to break out into song. No man had ever felt so good inside of me, and I wasn't sure if it was just because I was so damn attracted to him or because of our connection. I decided that it was probably a combination of both and focused my energy on the plethora of feelings exploding inside my body. Every touch of his fingertips drove me mad. Looking into his eyes had me swimming in a sea of blue. I was lost in him, and I never wanted to be found.

"Julia." The sound of his breathy voice snapped me to attention, our bodies working in unison, grinding and lifting in perfect time.

"Yes?" I asked as his hand cupped my cheek.

"Tell me it's me for you. Just me and no one else ever again," he said before closing the small gap between us, his mouth enveloping mine.

I gave him my answer in that kiss, my tongue changing between hard and soft, docile and demanding, submissive and dominant.

His pace picked up, and I broke the kiss to watch the way his body moved—shoulders flexing, arm muscles bulging against his skin. I couldn't stop myself from reaching out to grab them, loving the way their hardness felt under my touch. Sensing that James was close to coming, I angled my hips up and watched as he came undone inside of me. And, as small beads of sweat dripped from his brow, he thrust into me one last time before collapsing, the full weight of him crushing me.

"James," I tried to say into his shoulder, "you're suffocating me."

"Shit. Sorry," he said before pushing himself down and resting his head on top of my stomach.

My fingers moved to his head and played with the strands of his hair as my heart beat like crazy inside my chest.

"I meant what I said. That wasn't just some heat-of-the-moment, passionate bullshit statement."

"I know you did." I grinned to myself, secretly loving the bits of alpha male he possessed when it came to me. It shouldn't turn me on, but it did.

He lifted his head. "Well?"

"Well what?"

"Is it just me from here on out?"

His head crashed back down, and I let out an oomph before I could answer.

"Yes, James. No one but you."

"Good. Because I have plans for us," he said against my belly.

I giggled, lost in the way his head bobbed with my laughter. "Plans, huh? What kind of plans?"

He shot up and gave me a look. "I'll tell you later. I want to show you something first."

"I've already seen it, if that's what you're trying to get at." I nudged my head toward the hard-on he was still sporting.

"That's not what I'm talking about, you little minx." He kissed my cheek and dragged himself out of bed. "Come on. Get dressed. I'll take you to eat after."

The promise of food after all the calories we'd burned was more than enough to get me to agree. "I love food."

"I love," he started to say before my body completely stilled, "food, too."

He finished with a laugh, and I wasn't sure if I was more relieved or disappointed. Realistically, I knew it was too fast for declarations of love, but our story wasn't typical, so the same rules didn't seem to apply.

WE WALKED OUT of my house hand in hand without a care in the world it seemed. James hadn't ducked out or snuck around the vines to avoid my father and his probable death if caught. We were out in the open, our blossoming relationship on full display for all to see. When we rounded the main house, we both stopped mid-step at the sight of our parents talking and laughing at the property line.

"Will we ever get used to seeing that?" I asked, wondering when that image wouldn't send a jolt of shock through my system.

"I sure hope so," James said in response. "But I'd be lying if I didn't tell you that my first instinct was to run and hide."

I laughed because my first instinct at seeing them had been to duck and slowly back away. Some habits were going to be tough to break. I couldn't wait until they were a thing of the past, something we looked back on and had to bring up to even remember.

"Think they'll retire sooner now that we're together?" James asked as we started walking again toward our families.

I smiled inwardly at how confident he'd sounded about us. He made me feel like, even though we'd just started, there would be no end.

"Probably not." I gripped his hand a little tighter as we neared.

The four of them turned at once to face us, smiles all around, even on my dad.

"Morning, you two," my mom said in greeting before giving us each a hug.

It was hugs all around, and even though it was weird as hell, it was also amazing.

"Where are you two headed?" James's mom asked.

I shrugged because I had no idea.

"I'm going to show her the barn." He kicked at some dirt on the ground, and tiny rocks scattered.

"Oh"—his mom clasped her hands together in joy—"she doesn't know, does she?"

My eyes pinched together as I questioned what kind of mom would be *that* excited over a boxing setup. "What exactly is in that barn? A full-size boxing ring? Do you have a secret boxing club that I'm being initiated into? I mean, I heard it's a good workout, so—"

"A what?" Mrs. Russo laughed, but her face was full of confusion. "Boxing?"

I had asked James once what was in the barn, and he told me that he boxed in there. I remembered that answer clear as day even if he had looked weird when he admitted it to me. He'd said he was boxing the night of the fire. I knew I hadn't heard him wrong, but now, I was questioning everything.

Suddenly, I got excited. "Wait! Is it a horse? My dad never bought me a horse even though I asked for one every year at Christmas. Top of my list each year. Number one request. We have the property for it and everything." I waved a hand toward our land. "But do you see a horse there? Nope. No horse. Santa hates me."

My dad crossed his arms and fought back a shit-eating grin. "We have land for growing grapes, not for growing horses. Do you have any idea how expensive and how much work a horse is? I always told you that once you got older, if you wanted one, you could get one yourself." He looked at James before laying a strong hand on his shoulder. "The horse wish now falls to you. Good luck."

James gave my dad a resigned look before he glanced at me. "We'll discuss the horse thing later."

I stomped a foot in a mock temper tantrum. "So, there's no horse in the barn?"

Everyone laughed, clearly entertained and amused by our antics, and I closed my eyes for a second to drown my senses in the new-to-me sounds and feel. Even the outside air had been altered by our war's end. Or maybe it was our collective new energy that had changed it all. Whatever it was, it was palpable. And so beautiful.

"I'm going to show her and then take her to breakfast. Would you all like to join us?" James asked politely.

I prayed our parents would say no. It wasn't that I didn't want them there; I just wanted to be alone with him.

"No, you two go ahead. We'll grab dinner in town this week," Mr. Russo suggested, and everyone agreed.

Our two families sharing a meal in public was going to be the talk of the town for weeks, if not years. It thrilled me to think that the town would finally have something positive to say instead of avoiding the thick, dark clouds that seemed to hover over us at every turn.

With my hand intertwined with James's, we walked in step toward the barn. He pulled open the door and ushered me inside as I looked around at the light-filled space. There wasn't a boxing ring or a boxing bag in sight.

Confused, I turned to face him. "If you don't box in here, then what do you really do?"

"I'm sorry I lied to you at dinner when you asked. I just ..." He walked quickly, and I followed right behind him, heading for the brightest area in the barn. It was in that moment that I saw the various easels, canvases, and paints set up. "Not many people know I do this, and I wasn't ready to tell you."

There were so many paintings—landscapes, grapes, still life, and objects. All done beautifully with a whimsical touch. Each one looked like it sparkled.

"You did all these?" I asked in awe. I'd had zero idea that James Russo could paint.

"Yeah. Are they stupid?"

He bit his bottom lip, and I wanted to wrap him in my arms and tell him that the last thing they were was stupid. *How could he question how amazingly talented he was?*

"Stupid? They're beautiful. They should be labels on every bottle of wine you sell," I said before leaning in close, admiring the way they shimmered, the sparkle catching your eye as you moved away from it, therefore drawing you back in. "They're magical, James." I turned to look at him, my hands cupping his face. "Seriously. Magical. And eye-catching. How do you get them to shimmer like that?"

"It's a technique I've always favored. I kept at it until I mastered it. You really like them?"

"Yes." I nodded like a bobblehead for emphasis. I couldn't nod fast or vigorously enough to make my point. "They should be labels. If you don't rebrand all your wine, they should definitely be on at least the limited-edition bottles. You could even market them as James Russo exclusives and sign each one." My mind raced with all the possibilities.

"Think you could help me with that? Sell the idea to my parents?"

"Of course! And, if they say no, we'll do it ourselves."

It was my turn now to convince James that what we had wasn't ending. We'd started a partnership I had no intention of leaving.

"We'll do what ourselves?"

"We'll make our own labels for a wine we create together," I said with a smile.

James reached for me, and his strong arms wrapped around my waist as he spun me in circles. "You want to create wine with me? Really?"

"I thought we were doing everything together now. I thought you said this was forever. Were you lying to me, James Russo?"

I leaned my body back in an effort to put space between us, but it didn't work. His grip on me only tightened.

"Nope. Just glad to hear you're on board."

He kissed me hard with a ferocity and possessiveness I never knew I craved. I leaned in, giving it back to him just as hard.

We broke away, both of us racing to catch our breaths and slow our heart rate.

"What about the rest of the plans you have for us? Care to share them with me?" I asked while still in his arms, feeling more emboldened.

"I'm not sure you're ready to hear them, but I might as well let you know anyway." He nipped at my nose, kissed my forehead, and tucked a long, dark strand of my hair behind my ear. "We're going to get married, merge our wineries, and become a powerhouse that no one can touch. Ever heard of the hashtag couple goals? That's going to be us in this industry and in life."

"We're going to get married, huh?" I pushed away from him and started pacing a little as my heartbeat sped up again.

"Not like tomorrow. Jeez, Julia. But, when we do, I was thinking the Russo–La Bella Winery has a nice ring to it."

My jaw dropped as a look of disbelief crossed my face. "No way. The La Bella–Russo Winery sounds far better," I argued before realizing what I'd done. "I mean, for marketing purposes. It flows. It just sounds better than the other way, is all."

James wasn't listening to me anymore. He had some dopey look on his face, lost in whatever scene was playing out in his head.

"Oh my God," I shouted, pretending to be offended, and he snapped out of whatever daydream he'd been lost in.

"What?" He crossed his arms over his chest as if to ask, *What now?*

"You're just using me for my south side vines, aren't you?"

"You'll have to marry me to find out."

"We should probably start dating first."

"Julia La Bella, always making me wait unnecessarily when the outcome will be the same, no matter what, but okay, we'll do it your way." He pretended to sound bothered, but I knew he wasn't.

My jaw opened wide as another thought flew into my already-overworked brain. "You're in on the town bet, aren't you?"

A loud laugh escaped him. "They won't let me bet!"

I laughed out loud, crouching over in half. "Did you try?"

"Of course I tried! Hell, even Jeanine and Dane tried to get in on it, but no close friends or relatives are allowed."

"This town." I shook my head in mock disbelief because I secretly loved it. The fact that there was a bet about me and James meant that they were rooting for us, and I liked knowing that everyone had been on our side all along.

FEED YOUR GIRL

James

JULIA'S STOMACH GROWLED, and she tried to cover it with her hand, as if that would somehow stop the sound from echoing in the all but hollow barn.

"Time for breakfast?" I asked.

"Obviously. Don't you know you need to feed your girl?" She stomped one foot on the ground.

"I do now."

I still couldn't get over Julia's face when she had seen my paintings. I had always loved them but had no idea if they were really something marketable or even remotely good. Dane's opinion never counted. Neither did my mom's because, well, they were both biased. Not that Julia wasn't, but I would have been able to tell if she was lying just by looking in her eyes. They gave everything away.

Those hazel irises were going to be my biggest ally for the rest of my life.

We headed into town, and my fucking heart raced at the thought of walking through the streets with her on my arm. And it had nothing to do with our family history and everything to do with me finally getting the girl I'd wanted my whole damn life.

"What are you thinking about?" Julia asked from beside me, her hand resting firmly on my thigh.

I glanced over at her before focusing back on the road. "Just how lucky I am. And how incredible it feels, knowing that I can be seen with you in public, and it won't start World War Three at home."

She blew out a breath. "Tell me about it. It's like we have a whole new life."

Reaching for her hand, I moved it to my lips and pressed a kiss there before putting it back on my lap. Navigating the busy streets, I found a parking spot right up front and chalked it up to the fact that as of last night, my luck had changed. Yes, I considered a primo parking spot good luck.

"Don't get out," I instructed my impatient girl as I exited the car and made my way to her door. Opening it for her, I reached for her hand and helped her out.

"Who knew you were such a gentleman?" She blushed as she straightened out her top.

"I'm not," I said before kissing her cheek. I couldn't keep my damn lips off this woman. "I'm only one for you."

"I don't hate that." She grinned and ran her fingers down my beard.

"Hey, Romeo and Juliet," Jeanine shouted.

We both looked up to find her and Dane waiting at the diner's entrance.

"What are you doing here?" Julia looked happily surprised as she sped up to greet her best friend with a hug.

"Lover boy told us to meet you guys. Said food was on him, and who am I to turn down a free meal?" she said before greeting me with a hug as well. "I think you did good," she whispered approvingly in my ear.

"I think so, too."

"Hey, buddy," Dane said as we shook hands like men before he pulled me into a bear hug.

"Did you put in our names?" I asked.

Dane said he did and that our table was ready.

The four of us walked into the diner, and I swore, time stood still. The sound of silverware clattering against plates met my ears as everyone turned to watch us. I squeezed Julia's hand a little tighter but realized that she didn't need the comfort.

My girl wasn't the least bit uncomfortable, and she proved it when she addressed the enamored crowd, "We're together, okay? You're all the first to know. Tell your friends. The feud is over. Right, babe?" she turned and asked me.

"Yep," was all I could say in response because I was so damn surprised and proud and turned on.

We slid into a booth as cheers and clapping erupted around us.

I heard a few things like, "It's about damn time," and, "Finally," and, "Did she say the feud was over?"

It should have been unnerving, having strangers and acquaintances alike treat us like we were some sort of celebrity couple, but the truth was that we were used to it.

We'd been the talk of the town since we were born, and having everyone up in our collective personal business was par for the course by this point.

Jeanine reached for the glass of water in front of her and sipped at it. "It was always fun, being in public with Julia before, but being in public with the two of you together is something else entirely," Jeanine added as she opened her menu.

"I like that we're famous by association," Dane said, and I kicked him under the table. "Ouch. Damn it, Russo, that hurt."

"No one is famous. It's just a small town with not much going on. This is a big deal right now. It will die down," Julia said, and I thought she actually believed it.

I knew that our story would never die down, and with each new milestone we crossed together, the town would be by our side, cheering us on. We'd been born into the kind of stuff that town legends and folklore were made of. Only now, our choices going forward would tell of our love story instead of our mutual destruction.

"Do you know what you're going to get?" I asked my girl as she read the menu. I never even needed to look; I rotated between three things each time I ate here.

She closed her menu and placed it on top of the table. "I really want waffles. With lots of butter. And syrup. And I don't care if you look at me differently after I've cleaned my plate. Your girl likes to eat. Get used to it."

I threw my arm around her shoulders and tugged her against me. "I don't have to get used to it. I love it."

"You two are disgusting to be around, and you just got together." Jeanine pretended to puke.

"At least you're only having to deal with it now," Dane directly addressed her. "I'm sitting here, thanking God they're finally together, so I don't have to listen to him whining about not having her anymore."

I picked up my napkin and tossed it at Dane's head. "Can't fault me for knowing what I want. More than I can say for you."

"It's not my fault that all the girls in town suck," Dane complained. Jeanine made an offended sound. "Present company excluded."

"Apology accepted." She nudged him with her shoulder as the bell on the diner door jingled, capturing my attention.

I watched as Todd fucking Lestare made his way into the diner, alone. As the waitress walked him to his table, he noticed us and stopped following her, resting a hand on the edge of our booth.

"Well, well, well," he said, taking the four of us in before focusing solely on the arm I had wrapped around Julia's shoulders, "isn't this a surprise?"

My neck cracked as I jerked it from side to side, my body stiffening in response to his presence. I still hated the guy just as much as I had back in high school.

"Julia," he fucking purred. "Looking as beautiful as always."

This douche bag had just purred at my girl, and I felt my temper more than just rise; it shot through the damn roof and burned the town to the ground. I wanted out of the booth, but I was stuck between the wall and Julia.

My hands gripped the table, my body needing something to squeeze the life out of, as I ground out,

"Don't talk to her. I told you that back in high school, didn't I?"

He bit out a laugh. "We're a long way from high school, Russo. If Julia doesn't want me to talk to—" he started but stopped the second Julia stood up from the booth and got right in his face, her finger poking him in the chest.

"James told me what you said about me. He told me what you wanted back then. You're a pig. I've never been interested in you. And I've told you that a hundred times, but you never listen. And, now, I know why. I've always been some sort of game to you." Her tone turned icy cold. "I might not let my boyfriend hit you, like I know he's dying to do right now"—she glanced back at me, my eyes stone cold—"but I'm not above it." Julia stood tall, her posture defensive and a little scary, to be honest.

"You're wrong, Julia. Not about high school, but about now." He sounded less than convincing, and I knew he was only trying to save face in front of the other diner patrons.

Thank God Julia knew it, too.

"I don't think so. Stay the hell away from me, or next time, I'll let my man do whatever it is he's dreaming about doing to you."

I waited for Lestare to say anything in response, but he didn't, which was the smartest thing he'd ever done in his life; I was sure of it. We watched as he tucked his tail between his legs and skulked away, mumbling to himself.

She slid back down next to me, and I practically came undone. My girl was a motherfucking spitfire. I still had so much to learn about her.

"Holy shit, babe. I'm so turned on right now. I might give the whole town a show. That was so hot."

"Please reward her later while I'm not sitting right here and forced to watch," Jeanine begged. "But that was totally badass." She threw her fist in the air, and Julia bumped it back with a smile that took up her whole face.

"Remind me not to mess with you," Dane said as he finished off his glass of water.

Julia acted like nothing had just happened. "Does everyone know what they want? 'Cause I'm still starving," she asked, and we all shook our heads in unison.

We ordered our food, and the waitress gave Julia a slick high five under the table where no one else could see. Apparently, Todd had taken her virginity back in high school and then never spoken to her again. She said she always wanted to spit in his food whenever he came in here but claimed she never followed through. I gave her permission to do it this time.

Julia and I filled our mutual best friends in on what had happened the night before with our parents, including details about the bet since Jeanine had never known the full story. Dane gave me a know-it-all look when he learned that he had been right all along in assuming that Julia really hadn't known about it. I kicked him once more under the table for good measure.

"Stop kicking me," he groaned, reaching under the table to rub his shin.

"Stop annoying me," I taunted.

"I'm so happy that we can be done with all the hate," Jeanine announced.

I suddenly realized how hard it must have been for them to be our closest friends. They'd been thrust into a war they had nothing to do with and forced to pick a side.

I was about to thank them for putting up with us when our waitress appeared and started distributing our food. All other sounds died as we dug into our respective breakfasts, appreciation escaping all of our lips. You would think we hadn't eaten in years. I watched Julia eat every last bite of her enormous waffle, just as she'd promised she would. It was a total turn-on, seeing a woman enjoying her food. The cutest part might have been when she spilled syrup on her shirt. She cared for all of about two seconds before shrugging her shoulders at me and forking another bite into her mouth. I laughed and swore I had fallen more in love with her in that moment.

After breakfast, I paid the bill, and we walked outside after answering questions from each person in the diner on our way out. Most of them congratulated us, told us to extend the happy thoughts to our parents before commenting on what a *lovely* couple we made.

"Should I come get my car?" Julia asked, looking between me and Jeanine.

Jeanine spoke up, "Nah. You ride home with lover boy, and I'll drop your car and things off."

"Are you sure? How will you get back home?"

She cast a nod in Dane's direction. "This guy's offered to take me."

"Okay then"—Julia grinned at her best friend before giving me a questioning look—"if you're sure."

"Oh jeez, you two, go away." Jeanine swatted Julia's arm, and we laughed before heading toward my car.

I walked to the passenger side, clicked the button on my remote, and went to open her door when the sound of someone shouting our names stopped us both.

"Julia! James! Wait!"

"It's Ginny Stevens," Julia said at the same time I realized who it was.

I wondered if she was going to ask us about our dinner from the other night or if she had an actual business question for us.

We stood still and waited for her to reach us.

"Hi there! I just came to see for myself." She looked down at our hands, which were not clasped. "Is it true?" she asked, her eyes wide as she waited for an answer.

She hadn't come to talk about wine at all. She'd come to have something to gossip about.

"Is what true?" I pretended not to know what she meant.

"James Russo, is it true that you and Julia La Bella are officially a couple? Did you come out to the whole town during breakfast at the diner? Make some declaration of your love before stringing Todd Lestare up by his balls? Gosh, I wish I could have seen that," Ginny talked a mile a minute, her eyes as wild as her hair. "Never did like that boy much. Why couldn't you have made this declaration at my restaurant? Would have been good for business."

"Sorry, Ginny. We'll make sure our first family meal is at your place, okay?" Julia answered for us both.

"You mean, the Russos and the La Bellas at one table? Together, without killing each other?" She clasped her hands together in delight.

"Yep."

"Oh, that will be just perfect! I forgive you both." She gave us each a squeeze before remembering why she'd come over in the first place. "Wait! You didn't answer me. Are you together? I need to hear it for myself."

"We most definitely are," I answered before pulling Julia into my arms.

"Yes!" Ginny thrust her fist in the air. "I won! I won the bet and all the money! I knew I'd win! I knew you two wouldn't let me down!"

"Glad we could be of service," Julia said with a laugh.

Ginny walked away, singing, "I won, I won, I won."

But I knew what the real truth was; I was the winner in this scenario.

I got the girl.

After all this time, I'd finally gotten the girl. And nothing and no one would ever change that.

EPILOGUE

Julia

JAMES PROPOSED LESS than a year later, claiming that we'd wasted so many days being apart that he didn't want to waste any more. I refused to argue with his logic, especially when I wholeheartedly agreed with it. People always said that when you found the right one, you just knew. And James and I both knew.

Once we'd mended the feud between our families, it was full steam ahead—in life, in our careers, and in love. Everything we'd been denying our entire lives went up in flames, and a new passion ignited in its wake. The town practically threw a party in our honor—not only for the war ending, but also for James and me finally "doing the damn thing." Ginny made sure that everyone knew she'd won the bet.

The proposal was romantic, sweet, and so very James. He set the whole thing up to look like it had that night back in high school when he *apparently* confessed his feelings for me, and I *allegedly* broke his heart. Since I had very little recollection of the entire evening, I didn't take full responsibility for it, torturing him every time he brought it up.

"I needed a do-over with a way better ending this time," he said as he led me to a blanket on the ground, surrounded by four empty wine bottles scattered at our feet.

I laughed, completely clueless as to what he was about to ask.

He got down on one knee, between rows of vines, my hand in his, and promised I'd remember it all this time. But I didn't. Because, when the man you loved more than anything in the world got down on one knee and started saying all sorts of beautiful things, your brain couldn't hear them all. It was like I stopped processing any sounds, and all I saw was a sea of blue and all the hope they held. I could tell you every single color and shade in his eyes before

I could tell you even a fraction of what he said to me that day.

But I did remember saying yes.

Distinctively.

Confidently.

And without a second thought.

"Yes, yes! A million times yes!" I shouted as he jumped up, still holding on to my left hand.

"This means forever," he said as he slipped the antique platinum and diamond ring on my finger.

"I wouldn't take a single day less," I said before his mouth hungrily captured mine with so much love and lust that I thought we might set the vineyard aflame.

WE PLANNED ON getting married right on top of the property line that currently divided the Russo and La Bella land. We wanted to start our legal lives right between the two vineyards, him standing on my side of the land and me standing on his. It felt symbolic to unite as one in the exact place that had torn our families apart for so long. James and I were merging, and soon, the land would as well. There would be no more division—not in name, property, or family.

The reception would be held inside the barn. Both of our moms had gone wedding crazy, stringing up tiny white lights in the rafters and drying fresh wildflowers and hanging them all over the place even though the actual wedding was still months away. It looked like a scene straight out of the movie *Sweet Home Alabama.* I had to admit that I loved it though, and it inspired ideas for how I could decorate the barn in the future once James and I officially took over.

"Think they're ever going to retire?" My fiancé wrapped his arms around me from behind and kissed the back of my neck.

"Probably not."

"Maybe, if we give them grandkids, they'll go away." He laughed against my ear, nibbling on the lobe, and I maneuvered out of his grasp before turning to face him.

"I think having grandkids will have the exact opposite effect. They'll never leave then."

He looked down at me, a gleam in his eye. "We'll just tell them that they can't see the kids unless they retire. That good grandparents don't work and should spend all their time babysitting and playing with their grandbabies."

I swatted his shoulder. "You're awful. But I like your style. And kids—with an S? How many babies do you think I'm popping out for you?"

His face lit up as he said, "Like, five." He patted my belly, and I had no idea if he was being serious or not.

"Five?" I choked out, half-terrified and half-excited by the idea.

Being an only child had been sort of lonely, and I always wanted siblings. A big family sounded really nice.

"I guess we could start with three." He pretended to be disappointed, and I rolled my eyes and shook my head.

Deep down, I knew that I would give my man anything he wanted and that five kids, even though it sounded completely overwhelming and insane, might be exactly what he ended up with. Only time would tell.

"I'm going to go check on the wine." I gave him a quick peck on the lips before heading into the bottling building on the La Bella side.

James and I had so many plans when it came to the vineyards and our wine. I'd ended up doing a ton of market research and come to the conclusion that merging our two already-successful wineries into a single one wouldn't be the smartest financial decision at this point or anytime in the future. We planned on continuing to bottle each vineyard separately but to also create various limited-edition blends under our brand-new label, La Bella–Russo.

It seemed like the smartest idea was to have three different wine labels for sale and distribution as opposed to only having one. Our first red blend combining the two wineries was currently aging, and I knew that even though I wasn't supposed to play favorites, the La Bella–Russo label was going to be my pride and joy. I smiled to myself, lost in thought about all that our future held as I made my way over toward the wine barrel aging my most recent creation.

James and I had talked endlessly about all of the buildings on our respective properties and how we were going to handle them once our parents finally handed us the keys to the castle, so to speak. After the wedding, we planned on living together in my bungalow until it was time to take over. Eventually, we would move into the main house on the Russo side since it had been recently remodeled and had the most bedrooms—six. If I was going to be popping out babies left and right, they needed somewhere to go, and the main La Bella house only had three rooms.

That made it the perfect place for our new tasting room. My old family home would be converted into one amazing tasting space for both wineries that included separate areas for hosting private parties and classes that Jeanine planned to offer on wine and food pairing. She also wanted to host bachelorette parties, bridal showers, and classes for couples only, and I told her that once it was set up, she could go wild. Speaking of wild, she and Dane had recently started dating after months and months and m-o-n-t-h-s of incessant and annoying flirting. James and I had been so relieved once Jeanine finally caved and asked Dane out, saying she was tired of waiting for him to take the hint already. Thank God he'd said yes.

I reached for a tasting glass before allowing a small amount of the dark red liquid to pour out from the barrel. I was nervous the blend still wouldn't be ready. Yesterday, it had been so close but not quite there. My mind drifted to the barn, and I saw my man sitting in his upstairs private painting studio, creating new beautiful pieces that we'd offer for sale in our gift shop below. I wondered if any of our future children would inherit his artistic talent.

Glancing at my workspace, I noticed the mock-up of a La Bella–Russo label I'd had done, featuring one of James's paintings. Just like I'd promised him, I was going to use his art for every La Bella–Russo wine, and eventually, I'd expand to put them on more exclusive items. No one loved his talent more than I did, and I wanted the whole world to see it.

Allowing the wine to sit for a minute, I sipped at it, realizing that a mere twenty-four hours had done the trick. It was darn near perfect. I absolutely loved the way it'd turned out.

My fiancé sauntered inside. "Is it ready?" he asked.

"Come taste for yourself." I held out the small sipping glass, and he took it, giving it a hearty swirl before drinking it all.

"Babe"—he poured himself more before swallowing it in one gulp—"this is epic."

"I know. It's really good," I agreed, knowing full well that this would win the next competition we entered.

"Did you name her yet?" He gave me a half-cocked grin.

"Sort of, but I wanted to run something by you first." I scrunched up my face and waited for his response.

"I'm listening," he said as he poured himself another half-glass, smelling and swirling it before drinking the whole thing.

"I was thinking that all of our La Bella–Russo blends should be named in honor of our old rivalry. A sort of homage to our families' history and all we went through to get to this point. Is that dumb?"

"That's brilliant. I love it. So, we could name them things like Romeo and Juliet or Bad Blood? Like that?" He started tossing out suggestions that I loved and would need to look up the legalities for before I could use them.

"Exactly like that."

"So, what name were you thinking for this?" He held his glass in the air, and I smiled wide in response.

"Bitter Rivals."

"Bitter Rivals," he repeated. "I love it. It's perfect."

I couldn't agree more.

THE END

Other Books by J. Sterling

In Dreams

Chance Encounters

10 Years Later: A Second Chance Romance

Dear Heart, I Hate You

The Game Series:

The Perfect Game—Book One

The Game Changer—Book Two

The Sweetest Game—Book Three

The Other Game (Dean Carter)—Book Four

A Serial Romance:

Avoiding the Playboy—episode #1

Resisting the Playboy—episode #2

Wanting the Plaboy—episode #3

The Celebrity Series:

Seeing Stars—Madison & Walker

Breaking Stars—Paige & Tatum

Losing Stars—Quinn & Ryson (Coming)

The Fisher Brothers Series:

No Bad Days—A New Adult, Second Chance Romance

Guy Hater—An Emotional Love Story

Adios Pantalones—A Single Mom Romance

Happy Ending

Thank Yous

Thank you to Michelle Warren for creating this beautiful cover- I absolutely love it! Jovana, thank you for editing your heart out – I know it was a mess. Lol And thank you to my beta readers; Krista Arnold, Denise Tung and Kristie Wittenberg – you came through so solidly when I needed you. Thank you for dropping everything and helping me out.

Thank you to all my "kittens" and to every one of you who happens to read my books. I'm so thankful and grateful. I know there are literally a bajillion books out there to choose from, but I'm so humbled everytime you choose to read one of mine. :)

Blake – you moved out and ditched me and I'm simultaneously happy and sad about it. But mostly I'm proud. I can't wait to watch you play baseball this year! And congrats on releasing your first poetry book – it takes guts to put yourself out there like that. I think you are so talented; I hope you don't ever stop writing, or chasing your dreams. I'm so lucky you're my son.

Brett – you came back into my life with a vengenance and a whole lot of lost time to make up for. I am obsessed with the way you love me. I hope you never stop. Thank you for choosing me. Thank you for inspiring me and listening to me and for helping me – even when I tell you I don't want or need your help. I'm stubborn sometimes and instead of getting mad, you simply

UNDERSTAND. I'm not sure what I did to deserve having you as my partner, but I'm never letting go. I love you. Fiercely. And forever.

About the Author

J. Sterling is a Southern California native who loves writing fun stories that you can get lost in and will leave you with a big smile on your face. She's a big believer in happily ever after, and hopes all of us find ours. She has her bachelor's degree in Radio/TV/Film and has worked in the entertainment industry the majority of her life.

J. loves hearing from her readers and can be found online at:

Blog & Website:

www.j-sterling.com

Twitter:

twitter.com/AuthorJSterling

Facebook:

facebook.com/AuthorJSterling

Instagram:

instagram.com/AuthorJSterling

If you enjoyed this book, please consider writing a spoiler-free review on the site from which you purchased it. And thank you so much for helping me spread the word about my books and for allowing me to continue telling the stories I love to tell. I appreciate you so much. :)

Made in the USA
Monee, IL
04 September 2022